Lynn quickly ... ... ng container.

It took her only a few seconds to pick the lock, then she eased open the door and stepped inside.

The container was packed with crates from floor to ceiling on either side of a narrow aisle. The packing invoices described the contents as pottery and glassware.

As she ran her scanner across one of the crates in the very back of the container, it lit up like a Christmas tree. She froze. No doubt about it, the reading was clear.

Breathing shallowly, she moved closer and saw there was some sort of timer on one side of the crate.

Bomb!

She'd found it.

"Nick, container 16002. The bomb's in here."

Out! She wanted out. She had to get out of here; her job was done.

She turned to exit just in time to hear the sharp bark of a dog. The door of the container crashed down. For a long moment, she stared at it in horror.

She was trapped.

Inside the container.

With the bomb.

Dear Reader,

There has often been a book I've read that I wished when I put it down I could revisit the characters a year later and see how they were doing. Did their dreams come true? Did their love last? For years I fantasized that Scarlett won back Rhett long after *Gone with the Wind* ended.

When I was asked to write *Pawn* with the same characters that had been in *Deceived,* I was thrilled to get the opportunity to see how Lynn and Nick were doing. As a writer it was both a challenge and a delight to work with these two characters again, and what a surprise to discover they didn't get their happily-ever-after that was hinted at in the end of *Deceived!*

I hope you enjoy their story and, as always, happy reading!

Carla Cassidy

Carla Cassidy

PAWN

Silhouette®

BOMBSHELL™

Published by Silhouette Books

America's Publisher of Contemporary Romance

Special thanks and acknowledgment are given to
Carla Cassidy for her contribution to the
ATHENA FORCE series.

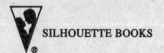 SILHOUETTE BOOKS

ISBN-13: 978-0-373-51412-0
ISBN-10:   0-373-51412-3

PAWN

Copyright © 2006 by Harlequin Books S.A.

www.SilhouetteBombshell.com

Printed in U.S.A.

Recent books by Carla Cassidy

Silhouette Bombshell

Silhouette Intimate Moments

CARLA CASSIDY

isn't a secret agent or martial arts expert, but she does consider herself a Bombshell kind of woman. She lives a life of love and adventure in the Midwest with her husband, Frank, and has written more than fifty books for Silhouette.

Chapter 1

Phoenix, Arizona

The police car had been following her for at least ten minutes before the cherry lights came on, flashing brilliant red glares across the stretch of desert on either side of the two-lane highway.

"Damn," Lynnette White muttered as she slowed her car and came to a halt just off the shoulder of the road.

She watched in her rearview mirror as the police car pulled up behind her and stopped. She didn't think she'd been speeding. She'd made no illegal turns and hadn't been driving erratically. So, why was she being stopped?

A burly officer stepped out of the driver's side of the car and walked with purpose toward her window. Maybe she *had* been speeding, she thought. She'd been known to have a bit of a heavy foot.

She rolled down her window and gazed up at the unsmiling man. His sunglasses gave away nothing, the mirrored surfaces reflecting the deepening shadows of the barren, brown landscape that surrounded them.

"License and registration," he demanded.

"Good evening, Officer. What's the problem?" she asked pleasantly.

"Ma'am, I need to see your license and registration." His stern features and curt tone radiated a no-nonsense attitude.

Lynn was tired and eager to get home to her apartment on the outskirts of Phoenix. She'd stayed at Athena Academy, the private girl's school, longer than she intended and now just wanted to get home. The last thing she wanted was to instigate any kind of hassle with the policeman that might hold her up.

She pulled her driver's license from her purse, then grabbed her car registration from the glove box and handed both to the man who was keeping her from her dinner and what little was left of the evening.

If she'd been speeding, she'd accept a ticket, pay the fee and that would be the end of it. Unfortunately it wouldn't be the first time she'd paid a speeding ticket.

She watched as he stared at her paperwork, then at her as if making certain the bad photo on her driver's license matched her face. She hadn't changed much since the photo had been taken. Her chestnut hair was a bit longer, but her eyes were still an unusual green-gold blend and her weight was the same, give or take a few pounds.

He looked back toward his patrol car and gave a nod, then opened her car door. "Ma'am, you want to step out of the car?"

Lynn frowned as her heartbeat increased. "No, I don't. Not until you tell me what's going on." She was aware of another policeman approaching them. "If I was speeding, just write me the ticket."

"This isn't about a speeding ticket, Ms. White," he replied.

What was happening? Her paperwork was all in order. "Then what is it about?" She was positive she'd done nothing wrong.

"Ms. White, we're under orders to take you into custody. Now, you can either make this difficult or you can make it easy, but one way or another, you're coming with us." As if to punctuate his sentence his right hand crept to the butt of the gun in the holster at his hip.

Lynn quickly considered her options and was smart enough to recognize she had none. She was still in the process of learning exactly what she was capable of, but she knew that despite her incredible genetic gifts, she couldn't outrun a bullet.

Unease whipped through her. "What about my car?" she asked as she stepped out into the hot, late-August air.

"Officer Birch will follow us with your vehicle," he replied and gestured to the second man who had joined them.

Lynn looked from one to the other, but their rigid countenances gave nothing away.

Heart pounding with anxiety, she grabbed her purse, handed Officer Birch her car keys, then headed toward the waiting patrol car.

Minutes later, as she was driven to an unknown destination, she wondered if it was possible that the sins of her past had finally caught up with her.

It had been over a year since she'd stopped breaking a hundred laws all in the name of love for her godfather, the man she'd called uncle, Jonas White. Of course, at the time she hadn't realized she was breaking laws and she'd been naïve enough to believe his lies.

For several years Lynn had been an expert cat burglar, breaking into museums and private residences to retrieve precious artifacts and jewels. Her Uncle Jonas had told her that they were working for the government, taking items that had been stolen so they could be returned to their rightful owners. But, in truth, she'd been stealing on Jonas's behalf for his personal gain.

When she'd agreed to work with the FBI to catch her godfather and put him behind bars they had promised that all pending charges against her would be dropped.

Had something gotten screwed up? Was there still something on her record that had alerted the Arizona cops to the crimes she had committed in Miami?

She worried a strand of her shoulder-length hair between two fingers. She hadn't felt this level of anxiety since discovering that the godfather who had raised her, the man she'd loved like a father, had been nothing more than a criminal using her skills for his own advantage.

A year ago the fates had taken away her support system, ripped apart her security, but in return she'd discovered that she had two sisters. Thoughts of Dawn and Faith and all the special women who had become her friends in the past year brought with them a surge of strength. Whatever was happening, Lynn would get through it.

Her stomach knotted as they pulled into a parking lot in front of a large warehouse. She sat up straighter. What was this? She'd expected a police station. This place was in the middle of nowhere. Something wasn't right here. Something definitely wasn't right at all.

There was also no way out of the backseat of the patrol car, which was apparently used frequently to transport criminals. There were no door handles on the inside.

She leaned forward to speak to the officer through the wire mesh that separated the backseat from the front. "Where are we? Why are you bringing me here?" Her anxiety toyed with becoming full-blown panic.

The officer's continued silence only increased the frantic flutter of her heart. He'd spoken only once during the ride, and that was to radio in to somebody that they were in transit.

A handful of cars were parked in the lot and as their vehicle came to a halt, the officer shut off the engine and turned in his seat to look at her. "Don't worry, Ms. White. You aren't in any danger."

"Easy for you to say, you're in the front seat with a gun," she replied with more than a touch of nervous irritation.

As he got out of the car and opened her door to allow her to exit, she once again assessed her options. There was no doubt in her mind that she could outrun him. Lynn had never met anyone she couldn't outrun. But, there was the little problem of his gun.

She had no idea if he'd use it if she took off, but she wasn't willing to take the gamble. Besides, even though she was anxious about the whole situation, she had to admit she was also more than a little bit curious.

Curiosity killed the cat, she reminded herself as she stared at the cavernous building.

As the officer led her toward the front door, she was aware of Officer Birch arriving with her car. He parked it next to the patrol car.

Dusk had disappeared, replaced by night and a

darkness that made it difficult for her to discern exactly where they were. Heat radiated from the pavement as she was escorted between both officers across the parking lot. Her heart pounded.

A tall, silver-haired gentleman in a dark suit met them at the door. "Thank you, Officer Cook, that will be all." The officer who had initially stopped her turned on his heels and headed back toward his patrol car.

The dark suit said nothing more until Officer Birch handed him her car keys. Once that policeman had left them alone, the man looked at her. "Ms. White, thank you for your presence."

"I didn't exactly have a choice, did I?"

He smiled, a smooth, practiced gesture she instantly didn't trust. "I'm Special Agent Samuel Cahill with the Federal Bureau of Investigation. We'd like to talk to you." He gestured her through the door.

FBI. She should have known. Her heart hardened. They'd used her once before and there was no way she intended for them to ever use her again.

"I'm not interested in anything you'd like to talk about," she said and remained standing at the doorway.

A flash of annoyance crossed his features, there only a moment then gone beneath a pleasant facade. "Please, Ms. White. It's a matter of great importance. If you'll just give us a few minutes of your time you can get back on the road again."

I don't want to do this, Lynn thought even as she

nodded her reluctant assent. There is no way they're going to suck me into doing anything for them.

She stepped through the doorway, surprised to see that the building appeared to be a temporary headquarters of sorts.

Bright lights illuminated desks where several men sat either talking on the phone or working on computers. Electrifying energy filled the air despite the evening hour of the day.

It was obvious something was amiss, but no matter what it might be she couldn't think what any of it would have to do with her.

"If you'll just follow me," Samuel said and led her past the desks and toward an inner office where blinds were pulled down and the door was closed.

A terrible dread filled her as she approached the office.

For the last year she'd rebuilt her life, a life that had been shattered beneath deception and lies. She'd moved from her godfather's luxurious mansion on the beach in Miami to a small apartment in Phoenix. She'd made a nice life for herself here and she wasn't about to let the FBI ruin things for her.

Whatever they were selling, she wasn't buying.

Samuel opened the door and motioned for her to precede him. She stepped in to find a man seated behind a large desk.

He was an odd-looking man with an unusually wide forehead and a small nose. His buzz-cut hair looked unnaturally black and his eyes were that pale blue color that never managed to look warm. He stood, his gaze sweeping over her with intense assessment.

Every sense that Lynn possessed went on high alert. She knew instinctively that this was not a man to screw with. An aura of power clung to him, nothing subtle about it.

"That will be all, Agent Cahill," he said.

Cahill dropped Lynn's car keys on the desk, then nodded, left the room and closed the door behind him.

"Ms. White, I'm Special Agent Richard Blake. Please, have a seat." He gestured to the chair in front of the desk. When she was seated, he eased back down behind the desk and eyed her with open speculation.

Once again an overwhelming sense of disquiet fluttered through Lynn. Who was this man and what did he want from her? Although she had a million questions, she refused to give voice to a single one. She'd wait until he was ready to tell her what the hell this was all about.

She didn't have long to wait. He leaned forward in his chair, those pale eyes of his holding her gaze intently and radiating with keen intelligence. "Ms. White. We need your help."

"Why not just give me a call and arrange an appointment instead of having me dragged here off the street by some of Arizona's finest?" She didn't try to hide her irritation.

One of his dark eyebrows drew upward and a disbelieving smile curved his thin lips. "And had I called you to arrange an appointment, you would have come?"

"Probably not," she answered truthfully. The less polite answer was *not in a million years.* "Look, I don't want to waste any of your time or mine. I can tell you right now that whatever you want from me, I'm not interested."

"But you haven't heard what I have to say."

"It doesn't matter what you have to say," she replied. "I did my time with the FBI last year when I helped gather evidence against my godfather. It's not my fault he escaped arrest, and he's dead now anyway. I have no interest in disrupting my life to work with the FBI again."

"This is bigger than the capture of one criminal."

"It doesn't matter how big it is, I'm simply not interested." She stood.

She'd been curious when the cops had pulled her over and they had acted out of character. She wasn't curious any longer. She was just tired and wanted to go home.

"I paid my dues, Mr. Blake. A year ago I did what I could to help the FBI. Now I deserve to be left alone." She didn't want to hear what he had to say, what he might want from her. She was terrified of getting sucked into a drama she didn't need or want in her life. It was better to walk away knowing nothing.

"Sometimes we don't get what we deserve," he countered.

Lynn had enough. "Am I under arrest?"

"Of course not."

"Then give me my car keys. I'm out of here."

There was a split second when she thought he wasn't going to comply. She saw something dark and angry flash in the depths of his cold blue eyes, but after a moment of hesitation he held out her keys.

She snatched them from his hand, overwhelmed with the need to get out of here, to escape this man, this place. "Thanks, and I hope we never meet again."

She couldn't get out of the office fast enough. She looked neither right nor left as she walked back down the hallway toward the exit.

As she left the building the night air embraced her, but she was unsure if the heat was from the outside temperature or the edge of anger that stirred inside her.

She strode to where her car had been parked and didn't feel quite safe until she was behind the wheel with the doors locked. She couldn't quite believe how easily he'd let her go.

It took her only minutes to orient herself as to where they had taken her and get back on the highway that would take her home. Home to her apartment on the south side of Phoenix.

The small apartment was a far cry from the mansion where she'd been raised in the lap of luxury. Her Uncle Jonas had kept her isolated from friends but had made sure she had the best of everything that money could buy. She'd also been raised to believe she was the heir of wealthy parents who had died in a tragic boating accident.

Lies. All lies. She clenched her fingers around the steering wheel as she thought of the lies that had filled her life.

When the FBI had gone after Jonas and frozen his accounts, Lynn had discovered she had no trust fund. She had nothing. She hadn't cared, because she thought she had Nick. As always, thoughts of FBI Special Agent Nick Barnes brought with them a deep regret, an ache of love lost.

Nick Barnes had worked for her uncle. Of course, neither her uncle nor she had known that he was an undercover FBI agent determined to bring Jonas down. In the course of his investigation he and Lynn had fallen in love, but the timing for that love had been all wrong.

Lynn had just discovered the beginnings of the truth of her birth and the surprising existence of two sisters. One, Faith, lived in Louisiana where she worked in the evidence department for the New Orleans police. The other, Dawn, traveled the world on all kinds of hair-raising missions as some sort of mercenary soldier, fighting for justice. Lynn, left Miami and Nick behind to come to Phoenix to find out more about herself and the special school, Athena Academy, that their biological mother had attended. She'd known then that she couldn't go forward in her relationship with Nick until she had the answers she so desperately needed.

As she drove she began to relax. Driving had always been the way she unwound when she'd been younger. The only difference was when she'd been living with Jonas she'd driven a new model red convertible with all the bells and whistles.

She now drove a five-year-old sports car with a dented front fender, but she'd paid for it with money she'd earned and nobody and nothing could take it away from her.

She breathed a sweet sigh of relief as she parked in front of her apartment building. She'd half expected to be followed home, but had seen no suspicious cars behind her.

Familiar scents greeted her as she walked into her apartment. A trace of her perfume lingered in the air, mingling with the orange-scented furniture oil and the fragrant candles she loved to burn in the evening. The decor was simple, but suited her. She'd chosen earth tones in keeping with this desert place, much different from the lush tropical colors of the Miami mansion she'd shared with Jonas.

She dropped her keys on the desk in the corner of the living room, then headed for the kitchen and leftover pizza from the night before.

She zapped the pizza in the microwave, snagged a cold beer from the fridge, then sat at the table to enjoy her meal. But any peace the day had brought to her earlier had been destroyed by the unexpected events at the end.

What had they wanted from her? It was important enough that they'd hunted her down, pulled her over and brought her in. They apparently knew her mind-set well enough to understand that she wouldn't have come in to see them on her own.

Dammit, she had earned the right to be left alone. Even though she had known Jonas was a criminal, even though she had known he needed to be put behind bars, one of the most difficult things she'd ever done was agree to help the FBI put him there.

Pizza half-eaten, she got up from the table and carried her beer out to the back patio where the night sky was filled with a million stars.

When she'd first come to Phoenix over a year ago, she'd been on a quest to learn the truth about who she was and where she'd come from. What she'd discovered about her beginnings was like something out of a science fiction movie.

Her past included a murdered mother, a secret lab with human experimentation taking place and enough conspiracies to make her head spin.

But, in addition to the horrors she'd learned of, she'd also been united with two sisters who, like her, were part of an experiment, all three genetically enhanced with special gifts.

She upended her bottle of beer and took a deep swallow. Damn the FBI and damn Mr. Richard Blake for making her think about things she didn't want to think about.

Her computer mentally called to her, reminding her that she'd promised to have the Chastain Pharmaceutical Company Web site done in a month and it was a huge job. It was easy to lose herself in work, and that's just what she needed to banish all thoughts of the FBI.

She carried her beer back into the house and went into the spare bedroom, which she used as an office. In the past year she'd gained a reputation as a top quality Web site designer and had managed to earn a living by using her computer skills. It was a job she enjoyed and that allowed her to pick and choose the hours she worked.

As she waited for her computer to boot up she leaned back in her chair and closed her eyes, willing away the headache that niggled at the base of her skull.

The day had begun so well. She'd had lunch with Kayla, a friend of her late mother's, who served as police lieutenant of the small town of Athens, Arizona. Then Lynn had driven out to Athena Academy and had walked the grounds of the school where the mother she never knew had once walked.

Visiting the state-of-the-art college prep school nestled at the base of the White Tank Mountains brought a comforting peace to Lynn. It was a place of connection for her, a piece of her mother's history that Lynn cherished. She loved seeing the new science wing, which has been completed over the summer. Another friend of her mother's, TV news reporter Tory Patton, had given the dedication speech at the ribbon-cutting ceremony in July. Lynn had visited with more of her mother's dear friends afterward.

She'd never meant to make her home here in Phoenix, it had just happened. She'd always intended to return to Miami and Nick. When she'd first left him to seek the pieces of her life that had been missing, they'd managed to call and e-mail each other frequently. But, time had a way of slipping by and long-distance relationships rarely had a chance of working.

There had been no bitter blowup and destruction of her relationship with Nick, only the interference of different lives and different paths.

She frowned, blaming the unexpected appearance of the FBI for the whisper of regret that now filled her heart.

With her computer up and running she decided to check her e-mail before she got to work on the drug company's Web site. She pulled up her e-mail program and typed in her password.

Her mailbox showed about two dozen new e-mails. Several she knew were work related, a couple were from cyberfriends, some spam that had managed to get past her filters, but there was one sender she didn't recognize.

The return address read, Delphi@orcl.org.

Lynn frowned, trying to decide if she should open it or not. She had filters and blocks on the system that shouldn't allow in any viruses or bugs, but she also knew she couldn't be too careful.

Deciding to take a chance, she opened the message.

Athena sister Lynette,
You have come to our attention. Your special,

genetic skills are needed in our battle. As friends of Rainy we need your help. The Oracle Network awaits you. We will be in touch.

Lynn stared at the note, her mind whirling. Delphi...Oracle...sounded like something from Greek mythology. It would be easy to dismiss the note as nothing but some sort of crazy ad campaign or spam except that it mentioned Athena, her special, genetic skills and the mother Lynn had never known.

There were only a handful of people who knew that she had been created by a human experiment, that the experiment had been a success in that she had been born with superhuman speed and hearing and other strengths.

Even Nick hadn't known the entire truth about the circumstances of her birth and her full capabilities, although he had suspected she was physically gifted.

So, who had written the note and what was Oracle? She hit Reply. What is Oracle, she typed in, then hit Send. It took only a moment for her to get a message that the e-mail address of Delphi@orcl.org was not a working address.

"Curiouser and curiouser," she muttered. She spent the next half an hour trying to trace the e-mail address but came up with nothing. Definitely intriguing, but also rather suspicious.

Was it possible the note was from the FBI? She narrowed her eyes and stared at the message. It was pretty coincidental that she'd been detained by them earlier then came home to find this cryptic e-mail.

She closed the message, but was unable to still the new edge of agitation that rose up inside her. She didn't like things she didn't understand, things that didn't make sense.

And she got the definite feeling that somehow the peaceful, quiet life she'd built here was about to explode.

Raymore, Florida

The ring of the telephone pulled Nick Barnes from the sofa, where he'd been cat napping for the past thirty minutes. He gazed at his watch and frowned. Who in the hell would be calling at midnight?

He grabbed the receiver. "Hello?"

"Is Haley there?"

Nick's gut twisted at the sound of the deep male voice. "Sorry, you've got a wrong number."

"I was just looking for Haley."

"Nobody here by that name." He hung up the phone, his heart pounding with apprehension. Something was wrong. Otherwise he wouldn't have gotten that phone call.

He got up from the sofa and grabbed his car keys from the kitchen table, then walked down the hallway and paused in the master bedroom doorway. Good, the phone hadn't awakened her.

As he walked back down the hall toward the front door, he wondered what in the hell had happened. Whatever it was, it couldn't be good.

They had agreed, when he'd gone deep under-cover three months ago, that there would be no contact unless it was a dire emergency. The fact that the code had been used meant something terrible had occurred and that couldn't be good news for him.

He left a note on the table that said he'd gone to get a pack of smokes, just in case she woke up and wondered where he was.

As he left the house, as always, his gaze shot up and down the street, looking for anything suspicious, anything or anyone that didn't belong.

Although Raymore, Florida, was only an hour's drive from Miami, it was light-years away in culture and flavor. Struggling economically the small town was populated by people on their way down rather than on their way up.

It was also the place where an FBI undercover op-eration had been ongoing for the past year to break up a huge methamphetamine ring.

Nick started the engine of his ten-year-old sedan, then pushed against a panel in the door that opened to reveal a secret compartment. Inside the secret compartment was a cell phone.

As he headed away from the small bungalow he'd called home for the past three months, he punched in the number that would connect him with his contact.

"Are you safe?" a deep, male voice asked.

"I don't know. You tell me." Nick didn't know the name of his contact, had only spoken to him by phone once before, on the day he'd gone undercover. He knew the man only by his contact name of Haley, a name that would have nothing to do with his real one.

There were only three people who knew where Nick was and what he was doing in Raymore. Buzz Cantrell, an agent who coordinated much of the undercover work within the agency; Frank Jessup, Nick's boss; and Haley, a faceless voice over the phone.

"I'm alone in my car, on my way to a convenience store for a pack of cigarettes. What's up?" Nick's stomach remained knotted as he waited to hear what could only be bad news. As he listened to what Haley had to say, the knot twisted tighter. By the time Haley had finished telling him why he'd called, Nick had arrived at the convenience store.

Nick disconnected the call and sat for a minute, trying to digest what he'd just heard. He didn't want to do it, but knew the men in charge would find a way of forcing his hand no matter how much he protested.

He got out of the car and went into the store. As he paid for a pack of cigarettes, he continued to think about what he'd just been told. They were asking him to play a dangerous game. They couldn't pull him off the case he was working—too much time and effort had gone into setting him up in his current position.

But, they needed him to do another job for them, one that could not be done by any other agent. It was a dangerous request, with dangerous consequences should it be discovered.

He already knew that one false move on the case he was working would see him dead. The meth operation was headed by a handful of ruthless, amoral men who would think nothing of putting a bullet through his head should they entertain even a moment of suspicion. Now he'd been ordered to risk compromising his position.

He got back into the car and restarted the engine at the same time he shook a cigarette from the pack. He hadn't been a smoker before he'd started this job, and he intended to quit as soon as this assignment was finished, but you couldn't go out to buy cigarettes and not smoke them.

As he headed back toward the bungalow, he thought again of what he'd just been asked to do. The only positive thing he had to focus on was that if this got him killed, at least he'd have an opportunity to see Lynn again before he died.

Chapter 2

Lynn was having a bad morning. Part of the problem was that she was trying to function on too-little sleep. Despite the fact that she'd tried to forget the unexpected appearance of the FBI in her life once again, she hadn't been successful.

She'd tossed and turned all night, cursing them even as she wondered exactly what they'd wanted from her. She'd finally fallen asleep as dawn was creeping into the bedroom, then had awakened just before ten and had forced herself out of bed despite a headful of grogginess. After two cups of coffee she'd felt better prepared to face the day.

She'd punched on her computer with the intention of working only to discover that the piece of technological machinery had gone wonky.

It booted up just fine, but before she could touch another button it began indiscriminately opening and closing programs one after another. Her dancing dolphin screen saver, WordPerfect, Free Cell, Excel—every program large and small she had ever loaded into the computer flashed on and off the screen in mind-boggling succession.

She stared at the screen, stunned, wondering what in the hell was going on. She punched keys, trying to gain control of the possessed computer, but it responded to nothing she keyed in.

What was happening? When she'd opened that crazy Delphi e-mail the night before, had it somehow infected her computer with a new kind of virus?

She was still seated in front of the computer screen when a knock fell on her door. She got up to answer, unsurprised to see her next-door-neighbor Leo Tankersly. He often drifted in and out of her apartment as if he belonged.

"Hey, Lynnie." He walked through the doorway and headed for her kitchen, where she knew he'd help himself to her freshly brewed coffee.

Leo had made it clear from the moment she'd met him seven months ago that he wouldn't mind if their neighborly relationship moved on to something more intimate.

She stood in the kitchen doorway and watched

him pour himself a cup of coffee. There had been times in the past seven months that she'd been tempted to let herself fall into a relationship with Leo, times when loneliness had made his attractiveness look appealing.

And he was attractive. He was a big man, with broad shoulders and a headful of long, blond hair that made him appear lionlike. He had the clear blue eyes of an Arizona summer sky and an easy nature that made him comfortable to be around.

He owned his own construction business, but was the least driven man she'd ever known. He worked when he felt like it, or when his cupboards were empty. For him, work was merely a means to an end, not a way of life.

What had kept her from falling into a physical relationship with him so far was the fact that, as handsome as he was, as sexy as he looked in his jeans and T-shirt, there were no sparks for her, none of the visceral pull that she'd felt only once before in her life for a man.

"You aren't speaking this morning?" he asked once he had his cup of coffee in his hand. He raised a furry blond eyebrow.

"I'm having a bad morning," she said, unable to stop the frown she felt tug across her forehead.

"How can it be a bad morning? The sun is shining, the coffee is hot and all is well with the world." He grinned, exposing slightly crooked front teeth.

Lynn's frown deepened. Leo was one of those people who never had a bad day. Laid-back to the point of being comatose, he never expected anything and therefore was never disappointed. He was at peace with the universe in a way Lynn often envied.

"Something's wrong with my computer."

"Something's wrong with all computers," he replied. "Too much, too fast isn't good for anyone. Technology isn't always a good thing."

"I'm serious, Leo," she said with a touch of impatience. She led him through the living room and to the tiny spare bedroom she used as an office.

Leo took one look at her computer screen's activity and whistled beneath his breath. "Wow, what kind of evil virus did you manage to pick up?"

"I don't know. I can't even key anything in to see if I can find the problem." Once again Lynn stared at her screen.

It was like nothing she'd ever seen before. It was at that moment a thought struck her. Was it possible her "friends" at the FBI had decided to wreak a little havoc in her life?

It would be relatively easy for one of their computer techs to transmit a virus via the Internet directly to her machine. Even though she had the latest in security features on her computer, she knew no security was fail-safe and the FBI would have viruses that had never been seen before in their little cache of surprises.

She couldn't imagine what they would hope to

gain by doing something like this, other than reminding her of how powerful they were.

"Have you tried shutting it off and rebooting?" Leo asked. "Maybe that will reset it or something." Lynn shrugged, leaned over and punched the button to shut off the power.

"And while we're waiting for it to cool down or reset or whatever those things do, maybe we should just take a quick tumble in the bed." He grinned at her. "You look tense. There's nothing like a full-body massage to relax you. I'll use my body to massage yours."

She laughed in spite of her frustration. "Leo, do you ever think of anything else besides sex?"

"Food," he replied. "Speaking of which, do you have any of those cinnamon muffin things you had last week? They were awesome."

"No. I haven't been back to the bakery since you polished off the last dozen."

"Then if you aren't going to offer me muffins, you should offer me sex." A wicked grin curved his lips.

Again Lynn laughed. "You might as well give it up. It's never going to happen."

He held up one of his large hands as if to stop her protests. "Never say never. Who knows what fate has in store, and never might be something very different tomorrow."

He took a sip of his coffee and eyed her over the rim of the cup. "Are you sure you're all right? You really do look tense."

Lynn leaned against the wall and sighed. "I didn't sleep well and then I got up to this computer problem." She couldn't tell him about the FBI. Leo knew nothing about her history and she liked it that way. A clean start, that's what she'd wanted when she'd decided to move to Phoenix.

"Unfortunately, I can't help you with the computer and as far as not getting enough sleep, my advice would be take a nap." He drained his coffee cup and they left the office and returned to the kitchen where he rinsed his cup in the sink and put it in the drainer to dry.

"Guess I'll head back over to my place. I just wanted to check in and see what's shaking."

"Absolutely nothing. If I can get my computer working again I've got tons of work to do."

"All work and no play make Lynn a boring girl." His blue eyes twinkled.

She flashed him a quick smile. "All play and no work make Lynn homeless and hungry. Now, get out of here so I can figure out what's wrong with my computer." She walked with him to her front door.

"Wanna share a pizza tonight?"

She considered it for a moment. She and Leo often ate together on Saturday nights. "I had pizza last night."

"What about Chinese?"

"I don't think so, not tonight. I'm really swamped. I'll probably just nibble on something while I work." Although she did have a lot to do, that wasn't the reason for telling him no.

She didn't feel much like socializing, especially since what she did feel was the presence of an insidious threat hanging over her head.

"If you change your mind, let me know," Leo said. "I'm going to be in and out all day, but just leave a message on my machine or call my cell."

"Okay, but don't count on it."

She closed the door behind him as he left, then returned to her office and booted up her computer. To her surprise everything came up normal. She had just begun running a diagnostic to see if she could figure out what had caused the earlier anomaly when a knock once again fell on her door.

Probably Leo again. She rarely had any other visitors.

"Leo, I told you I'm not going to bed with you," she said as she pulled open the door.

She stared at the tall, handsome dark-haired man at her door in stunned shock. "Nick." His name fell from her lips in a breathless whisper.

"Hi, Lynn."

The familiar deep voice washed over her. "Nick," she repeated and with utter abandon threw herself into his arms. Oh God, he smelled the same, a rich blend of minty soap and earthy cologne and his body against hers felt wonderfully magical.

It had been so long, so terribly long since she'd seen him and it wasn't until this moment that she realized just how much she had missed him.

His arms wound around her for one sweet moment, then he disentangled himself and took a step backward. "Can I come in?"

"Yes, of course. Please, come in. My God, I can't believe you're here." Her head reeled with his presence. *Nick.* It had been a year since she'd last seen him and the sight of him filled places inside her that had been hollow for so long.

She led him into the living room, wishing she'd dusted, regretting the fact that she hadn't put on any makeup that morning. She couldn't believe he was here in Phoenix, here in her living room.

As he sat on her beige sofa, she drank in the vision of him. There were subtle changes in him from the last time she'd seen him. His dark hair was longer and his face was thinner, giving his appearance a dangerous edge that hadn't been there before.

But, some things remained the same. His white dress shirt tugged across broad shoulders and his dark slacks fit nicely across his slim hips and muscular legs. His eyes were just as dark and gorgeous as she remembered, but at the moment they held no real emotion.

She sat on a chair opposite the sofa and continued to stare at him as if he were some apparition. She'd dreamed of him often in the past year and what she wanted more than anything at this moment was to be in his arms.

Did he feel it, too? The sparks that had ignited between them a year ago now simmered once again in the pit of her stomach, on the verge of a full-blown inferno.

"How have you been? What are you doing here? Are you working here in the Phoenix area? You look wonderful." Giddy happiness swelled inside her and for a moment she felt like the young, innocent woman she had once been.

"I've been all right." His deep voice resonated inside her. His gaze swept the length of her. "And you look great."

She ran a hand through her hair, once again wishing she'd put on makeup, taken a little more time with her appearance that morning. "Thanks," she replied.

"I understand you've been doing well, using your computer skills to make a living."

"I'm doing okay. Creative Communications is the name of my business and it's been growing by leaps and bounds in the last couple of months." Some of the giddiness she'd experienced only moments before dissipated somewhat as she sensed a distance in him.

"I'm glad you're doing well, Lynn."

The last of her giddiness fell away as he didn't quite meet her gaze. Just because she had held thoughts of him close to her heart since their separation didn't mean he'd done the same with memories of her.

He'd been her first lover and she'd always heard that women remembered their first. She certainly hadn't been *his* first, so maybe their relationship had never meant as much to him as it had her.

"Nice place," he said as he looked around the room.

"Thanks. The rent is reasonable and I like the general area." She leaned forward. "So, you didn't tell me. Are you working in the area?"

He looked at her then, and in his dark eyes she saw something that caused a faint cold wind to blow through her. "It's a little more complicated than that."

"What do you mean?" The beat of her heart, which had gone wild at the first sight of him now slowed to a dull thud of wariness.

For a long moment he didn't answer as he once again broke eye contact with her. Whatever he had to say, it was obvious he was reluctant. He finally looked at her and any happiness she might have managed to hang on to fell away as she saw the un-emotional, businesslike look in his eyes.

"They sent me here, Lynn," he said. "They sent me here from Miami to try to convince you to work for them."

"Then I guess that makes you a bastard," she exclaimed.

The very first sight of her had been like a punch in the gut. She was as beautiful—no, more beautiful—than she had been a year before.

There was a new maturity in her unusual gold-green eyes, a confidence in her carriage that spoke of an inner strength that had been undeveloped when he'd known her before.

She'd been an innocent, very young twenty-two a year ago. Now she looked like a woman who had taken control of her life and was comfortable with the direction she intended to go.

He'd seen the happiness that had lit her eyes when she'd first opened the door and looked at him and had fought against a responding burst of joy in himself. She had been a thing of magic for him for all-too brief a time and in the first second of seeing her he'd once again felt that stir.

He couldn't get caught up in the memories, in her. Things had changed and there were now powerful people playing significant roles in both their lives. Of course, she wasn't aware of that yet, but within minutes she would understand that it was useless to fight the inevitable, that she could either go along with the program or be destroyed.

"I guess that does make me a bastard," he agreed. "A bastard who is following orders."

What little happiness remained in her eyes instantly doused at his words. Her gaze narrowed and her expression went from warm to arctic cool. "So, you're here as a tool for the Feds to use against me."

She stood and walked over to the living room window, her slender back presented to him like a wall. Her tight jeans hugged the length of her slender legs and cupped the curve of her shapely butt. The blue top she wore had spaghetti straps, making him realize there was no bra beneath. He definitely couldn't allow his thoughts to go there.

"Go away, Nick. I already gave them my answer." The flatness of her voice cut through him like a knife.

The last thing he wanted to do was hurt her, but he was in a box, and whether she knew it or not, she was in one, too. It was a box where somebody else had drawn the boundaries and there was no escape.

"It's not that simple, Lynn," he replied.

She whirled around to face him, her eyes more green than gold and radiating with an anger, a strength he'd not have thought possible in her. "What's not simple? I told them no, and I'm telling you no. I'm not working for them and that's that."

"That's not true," he countered. He wondered what life had taught her in the past year. When they'd first become involved she'd been unusually naive, without the kind of experiences that taught character and strength and purpose. That had started to change when she'd learned of his true purpose in working for her godfather. Now he saw disillusionment shining from her unusual eyes.

He tamped down his regret. He was here to do a job and he couldn't allow emotion or memories to cloud the issue.

He stood. "They aren't going to let you go, Lynn. They need you, and what they need you for is in the interest of national security."

"I don't care why they need me. They can't make me go back to work for them." She swiped a strand of her shiny, reddish-brown hair behind an ear, a gesture he remembered that indicated stress.

"That's where you're wrong. They can make you.
These people who contacted you, they aren't your
ordinary Feds. They're hybrids, working for a
splinter agency but under the guise of FBI. Trust
me, these aren't people to screw around with."

He took a step toward her, unsurprised when she
took a step back, wary suspicion playing in her eyes.
He hated them for making him do this, for using him
to get to her.

"How did your computer work this morning?" he
asked. "Have any problems?" She stared at him, a
pulse beating rapidly in the hollow of her throat. "This
morning they gave you just a little taste of what
they're capable of. Maybe nothing else will happen
today, but maybe tomorrow or the day after, your Web
sites will begin to experience difficulties. Mistakes
will appear on sites you've already built, errors that
make you look careless, that make you look incom-
petent. And, that's not all they'll do to you."

Her gaze narrowed and the pulse in her throat beat
faster. "You might as well tell me all of it," she
finally said.

"They'll destroy what you've built with your
business, screw around with your finances to ruin
your credit. And if none of that works, they have
enough charges pending against you that they can
put you in prison and throw away the key."

She moved back to the chair opposite the sofa and
sat down hard. For a moment she stared at some in-
definable point just to the left of where he stood.

When she finally met his gaze, her eyes once again blazed with an anger that stunned him.

"You promised," she said, her voice low and barely audible. "You promised me that if I helped bring down Jonas, then all those charges would be dropped. That was the deal, that my record would be clean. So, you lied to me." Bitterness hardened her voice.

"No, *they* lied to *me*," he said. "At the time I told you that, that's what I was being told. We were both lied to."

She leaned back in the chair and released a weary sigh. "Why me? Why can't they get somebody else to do whatever it is that needs to be done?"

"I don't know," he said honestly. "They didn't tell me what they want you to do or why they needed you specifically to do it. They only told me it involved national security. My job was to come here and see that you understand that you have no alternative other than to cooperate with them."

Her hard gaze held his for a long moment. "How nice, that they could use the emotional baggage of my past to try to bend me to their will."

Nick drew a deep breath and swiped a hand through his dark hair. He didn't want to remember the passion that had once filled him for her, refused to remember the love he'd once felt for her.

There was no point in going back there. At the moment his life was more complicated than it had ever been. There was no place in it for memories, for emotional weakness, for Lynn.

"I didn't want to do this to you," he said. "I didn't want to be a party to screwing up your life, but I had no choice in this, either."

One of her chestnut eyebrows rose slightly. "And what are they holding over your head, Nick?"

His chest tightened as he thought of the threats that had been leveled against him, against what was left of his family. "I'm just doing my job."

"Just like you did a year ago?" Bitterness was once again rife in her voice. "Just like you were doing your job when you seduced the boss's daughter in order to get closer to the boss?"

Those had been Nick's orders when he'd been working undercover to bring down Jonas White. He'd gotten a job as head of security at the mansion where Jonas lived, but when it looked as though he was as close to the man as he could get, Nick's orders had been to get close through Lynn.

What had begun as a job had become much more. He'd found himself enchanted by Lynn's innocence, charmed by her humor and stimulated by her intelligence.

"You know better than that," he now said vehemently. "No matter what has happened since, I didn't pretend anything that I felt for you then. You knew what I felt for you was real, not just some assignment I'd been handed." He held her gaze intently. "You were the one who left, Lynn. You were the one who walked away."

She stood once again, her posture stiff and chin

lifted in defiance. "And you know there were things I needed to figure out, things I had to find out about myself and where I came from."

"I know," he said softly. "And that was then and this is now and one way or another, they're going to get you. You might as well make it easy on yourself and find out what they want."

He pulled a business card from his pocket and laid it on the coffee table between them. "There's a number written on this. It will ring directly to Mr. Blake, who is waiting to fill you in. Call him, Lynn."

She looked at the card as if it were a Gila monster that had crawled up on her coffee table and taken up unwanted residency. When she gazed at him he once again saw a steely core of strength shining from her eyes.

"Message delivered," she said, then shot a pointed gaze toward the front door.

There were a million other things he wanted to say to her, a hundred regrets he'd liked to have voiced. He wanted to tell her that thoughts of her had often played in his head, that he'd always hoped he would see her again.

He wanted to ask her if she'd come to terms with the pain of Jonas's betrayal, if she'd found all the answers she'd been seeking when she'd left him behind. And, he wanted to know who Leo was and had she meant she wouldn't sleep with him today, or she wouldn't sleep with him ever?

But, what was the point? He wasn't inviting

himself back into her life. He had a plane to catch and a shadow life filled with bad guys waiting for him.

"Despite the circumstances, it was good to see you again," he said as he walked toward the front door. She didn't walk with him, but remained standing by the coffee table.

He opened the front door then turned back to look at her, waiting to see if she was going to say anything more to him.

She didn't.

As Nick stepped out of her apartment and pulled the door closed behind him, he wondered what the agency wanted with her, wondered if he had just handed her a death warrant. Because he knew more than anyone that the men who wanted her played for keeps.

Chapter 3

She made the call two hours after Nick walked out her front door. It had taken her that long to process everything he'd said and everything she'd felt at seeing him again.

She knew he was right. If they wanted her, somehow, someway, they would get her. They could make her life miserable and still sleep well at night.

At four o'clock that afternoon she got into her car to head to a meeting with the enigmatic Mr. Blake. The last thing she wanted to do was give the FBI another minute of her life. But she wasn't stupid enough to think that she could fight them.

As she drove to the warehouse where they had

taken her the night before, she tightened her hands
on the steering wheel as she thought of the threat of
imprisonment.

Breaking and entering, theft of artifacts, grand
theft—there were a thousand charges they could use
to see her in prison until she was a very old woman.

She'd been promised that the charges would be
dropped if she helped get Jonas under arrest. She'd
upheld her end of the bargain, but apparently she'd
been the only one to do so.

Big surprise, a government agency had lied to her.
Once again she tightened her fingers around the
steering wheel as she thought of their broken
promises.

She consciously kept her thoughts away from
Nick. What point was there in indulging in what-
might-have-beens? He'd been right. She had been
the one to walk away and she couldn't harbor bitterness about the fact that their relationship had died
due to lack of nourishment and through long
distance.

It pissed her off that he'd been the messenger of
doom, that the FBI had guessed that, of all people,
Nick would be the only one to convince her to do
what they wanted.

It also upset her that seeing him again had sent
all kinds of memories crashing through her head,
memories she didn't want to indulge.

It hadn't been Nick who had convinced her to
make the call. It had been the fact that she knew he

was telling her the truth, that they would stop at nothing. They would follow through on their threats to destroy her professional life and to take away her personal life. They'd proven that by what they'd managed to do on her computer that morning.

She had no choice in the matter.

What she hoped was that she'd meet with Blake, hear the details of whatever they wanted her to do, then somehow talk her way out of it without any further repercussions.

As she drove through the desert landscape her thoughts momentarily drifted back in time to the lush flowers, bright colors and salt-scented air of Miami.

She'd lived a life of luxury in an oceanside mansion that belonged to her godfather, Jonas, but she'd experienced love in a small beach house that had belonged to Nick.

Two-fifteen Harbor Road. The address popped into her head unbidden. Did he still own that small white bungalow with the cheerful yellow trim? The place where she had fallen so helplessly, so hopelessly in love with him?

She unclenched her hands from the steering wheel. Love. As far as she was concerned it was vastly overrated. Jonas had professed to love her, but he'd thought nothing of lying to her and using her special gifts for his own means.

Nick had said he loved her, but she'd never been sure if that had merely been an illusion they had both shared for a brief period in time.

There had been a time in her life when she'd dreamed of a Prince Charming riding to her rescue, coming to take her away from the isolation and loneliness of her life with her godfather. In the past year Lynn had realized she didn't need a Prince Charming. She didn't need anyone riding to her rescue.

Her sisters and the women she now called friends had brought out in her an inner strength she'd never known she possessed. A strength she had a feeling she was going to need now more than ever.

She pulled up in front of the warehouse. Only a couple of cars were parked out front. Last night it had been too dark to notice much about the building, but now she saw an old wooden sign hanging from a large pole that announced the place had once been Carlos's Cactus Jelly and Candy.

The bright colors of the sign had long faded, blasted by the desert sun, grit and wind. She wondered what had happened to Carlos? Had his life and his business been interrupted by a lack of tourists and poor business sense or had the FBI swooped in on him as they had on her?

Her stomach knotted as she shut off the car engine and stared at the large structure before her. Nobody would ever guess that there was an FBI operation going on inside.

Once again a sharp edge of apprehension stabbed her. She got out of the car, suddenly eager to put an end to the speculation and know the answers as to why they were after her this time.

A new face met her at the door, a tall, slender man with unsmiling eyes who didn't ask her name or business, but obviously knew she was expected. Without a word he led her back to the office where she'd spoken with Richard Blake before.

Blake greeted her at the office door, his pale blue eyes as cold as she remembered. "Ms. White, it's nice to see you again," he said as he ushered her inside and closed the door behind them. "Can I get you something cold to drink?"

"No, and you can cut the pleasantries. We both know I'm not here because I want to be but rather because you boys don't play fair." She sat in the chair in front of his desk, filled with a new sense of anger, of outrage.

"We play the cards we have in our hands," he said smoothly and sank down at the desk. "You could have made this easier by speaking with me yesterday."

"I didn't know then that you were going to infect my computer with a bug, threaten to trash my professional life and see me in jail for charges that were supposed to have been dropped a year ago. Oh, and I'm just wondering, did you send me a weird e-mail, as well?"

He frowned. "I don't know anything about an e-mail, but I do know that one of our techs sent a little bug to you this morning to make you understand that we weren't just going to go away."

"Okay, you have my attention. Now tell me what

you want from me." Make it something easy, she thought. Maybe whatever they wanted from her, whatever they needed from her would take an hour, maybe a day, and wouldn't disrupt or destroy her life after all.

He leaned back in his chair, picked up a pencil and began to tap its eraser on the desktop. "As I'm sure you know, since 9-11 the top concern of this country has been national security, particularly securing borders, and the need to prevent another 9-11 from happening."

His words were punctuated by the faint *thunk, thunk, thunk* of the eraser hitting the desk. "Our agency works closely with Homeland Security."

"What does that have to do with me?" she asked impatiently.

"As I'm sure you know, we've managed to effectively tighten our airport security. Our borders are more heavily patrolled than ever in the history of our nation and the politicians have finally realized that funding is vital in our quest for national security." *Thunk. Thunk. Thunk.* The eraser tapped faster.

Lynn tamped down frustration, wondering when the hell he was going to get to the point? She fought the urge to reach across the desk and snatch the damned pencil from his hand. The tapping of the eraser threatened to make her crazy. And she was already feeling crazy enough without anything else making it worse.

"There's only one place that our security measures are relatively weak, one place that could be far too easily breached, and that's our international docks." To her intense relief he threw the pencil down and leaned forward, his gaze cold and intently focused on her. "And that's where you come in."

She stared at him blankly. Was he completely mad? What could she possibly do to ensure safety at the country's international docks? "I don't understand."

He sat back once again and drew a hand across his overly broad forehead, as if he might be suffering a headache. She hoped so. He was certainly giving her the beginnings of a head-banging ache.

"We have received some troubling chatter that indicates an al Qaeda terrorist attack is possibly going to take place around the end of this month or the beginning of next month," he explained. "The chatter is coming from a reputable source and our intelligence tells us that the attack will come in the form of a dirty bomb in a shipping container. We believe that container is coming ashore at the Stingray Wharf in Miami. Unfortunately, we don't have specifics on where exactly it will come from."

Lynn frowned. She knew of Stingray Wharf. It was a small wharf near the bigger port of Miami. She still didn't understand why she was here, what exactly they wanted from her. "If this is happening in Florida, then what are you doing here in Arizona?" she asked.

"We have other sensitive operations going on," he replied.

Once again she wanted to demand he get to the point, but knew instinctively that this was a man who was going to do things his way and she needed to be patient.

"Many of the bigger ports of entry have obtained special equipment to scan containers for radioactive materials," he continued. "Unfortunately the equipment is exorbitantly expensive and Stingray Wharf hasn't gotten it yet.

"The way the system works there is, shipping containers are removed from incoming ships and placed in a holding area. They are inspected and cleared only as they leave the holding area on trucks. That's what makes the system ripe for a breach. Many of those containers remain uninspected for months."

"Certainly unsettling, but I still don't see what you people want from me?"

Once again his gaze was intent as he stared at her.

"This is what we want from you. We want you to go to Stingray Wharf and get into those containers in the holding area and check the contents."

Lynn sat back in the chair and stared at him in disbelief. "Is this some kind of a bad joke?"

"Trust me. There is nothing funny about any of this. A dirty bomb would not only affect the immediate area around the wharf, but could have devastating consequences to the entire state."

"I understand that," she replied. "What I don't understand is why you people can't just go in and check the containers, find the dirty bomb."

"There are several reasons we can't do that," Blake said. "First of all, the security at the dock is provided by a private agency. While the agency and its workers were given initial security clearances, we'd need to do a more thorough security investigation before bringing them in on this. We simply don't have the time."

He picked up his pencil and tapped the eraser on the desk. "Secondly, it's imperative that the public doesn't get word of the potential devastation that could take place. We can't control the people who work for that agency. Equally as important is the potential for awkward diplomacy issues. The containers that come into the port come from all over the world. If we just go in and start ripping them open we could create all kinds of diplomatic nightmares.

He threw the pencil down, leaned back in his chair and eyed her intently "Trust me, we have considered all options for maximum success and minimal damage. We believe the best way to proceed for the least amount of collateral and diplomatic damage is for somebody to get in and out of those containers and check them with a handheld radiation detector."

"Okay, but why me? Why not get somebody from Miami? I'm sure you have agents down there."

For the first time since she'd arrived he smiled, a cold, bloodless gesture that did nothing to assure her. "We don't have an agent on our payroll who is as good as you at breaking and entering, picking locks and evading capture. Nobody in our employ has your particular skills, your unnatural speed and agility, your acute sense of hearing and other talents."

Although it shouldn't surprise her, it did, that they knew so much about her. "So, the skills I used to commit the crimes that could see me in prison for years you now want to exploit in the name of national security," she asked incredulously.

His smile broadened. "Exactly."

"And if I'm still not interested?"

The smile dropped from his face as if it had only been a desert mirage. "Then we'll pursue other means in order to make sure that you're cooperative."

Thoughts flew through her head. She could run. She could pack up and disappear, leave her life behind. She could take a new name and hide, but her life as she knew it would be over.

She'd have to leave her home, her business, leave behind the women who had become so important to her and never again contact the two sisters she had only recently discovered. What kind of a life would that be?

None at all. The only real option she had was to give them what they wanted.

"All we're asking for is a week, two at the most. Our

intelligence has been pretty specific as to the dates. Two weeks out of your life, then we're out of yours," he said. "I'll even see to it that the pending charges against you are dropped and your record is expunged."

"I've heard that before," she said dryly. She sighed. She'd do it, only because they'd left her no real choice in the matter. "So, what are the details? How is this going to work?"

"You leave here day after tomorrow. If the chatter we've picked up on is true, then we think the bomb will come into the country within the next week in order for them to hit by the end of the month or the first of October.

"We'll spend the next two days briefing you on the specifics and making sure you're up to speed. An apartment near the docks has been rented for you— you'll stay there during the day and work at night. You'll have a contact working as closely with you as possible."

Her head spun as he went through the details. "I want Special Agent Nick Barnes to be my contact."

A frown etched across his large forehead. "I'm not sure that's possible."

"You make it possible," she replied with a note of finality. If she had to do this, she wanted somebody she trusted in her corner.

Despite the fact that she'd been bitterly disappointed that Nick hadn't shown up at her apartment because he'd wanted to see her, but rather because he'd been ordered to gain her cooperation, she trusted

him as she trusted nobody else on the face of the
earth.

"You're obviously a man who makes things
happen, Mr. Blake. You make this happen for me. If
I'm going to do this for you, then I want Nick Barnes
as my contact."

"I'll see what I can do, but I can't make any promises." He reached into the top desk drawer and pulled
out a manila folder. "Inside here are aerial maps of
the Stingray Wharf area and the holding enclosure.
Study them, memorize them. Your life might depend
on knowing the information."

"I'm hunting for a bomb, I'd say the least of my
problem is knowing the area," she said.

"On the contrary, getting into the holding area
will be as dangerous as finding the bomb. There will
be armed men and trained dogs guarding the area.
Neither look kindly on trespassers."

Dogs. Lynn fought a shiver that threatened to
walk up her spine. She was terrified of dogs, a fear
that had found its birth when a friend of Jonas's had
come visiting with his poodle. The poodle had bitten
Lynn on the ankle. She'd rather face a gun than deal
with a dog.

It was only then that she realized exactly what
they were asking her to do. "Trespassers? Then I'm
guessing this search I'll be conducting isn't legal?"

Mr. Blake frowned again and leaned back in his
chair as a deep furrow tracked across his broad
forehead. "These are dangerous times and there

are instances when red tape and the rights of the people interfere with what is best for the country. We are circumventing the first two in order to accomplish the last."

"So, what I'm doing is illegal," she said flatly. How ironic was that? That the government was asking her to do exactly what they threatened to put her in prison for. She was going to break the law with their blessing. The means justified the end.

His blue eyes were flat, without expression as he looked at her. "Not only that, but if you're caught, we'll deny all knowledge of you and your actions. We'll remind the authorities of the current charges pending against you. We'll imply that you went back to your old ways, breaking and entering in an effort to steal for personal gain. You're on your own if you get caught."

It was at that moment that Lynn recognized why they needed, why they wanted her. Her background made her an easy patsy should she be caught.

In the eyes of the FBI, she was completely expendable should she fail.

It was after six when she headed back to her apartment. Despite the evening hour the heat of the day shot water mirages across the highway.

She felt as if the life she had built for herself was nothing more than a mirage and in the blink of an eye could disappear.

She'd believed what she'd made for herself here

in the Phoenix area was strong and safe and wonderfully normal, that it was a place, a life that nothing
and nobody could take from her.

She'd been wrong.

In two days she'd be in Miami again, doing work
that could get her shot by a guard, eaten by a dog or
blown to smithereens by some terrorist bomb. One
thing was for certain, during the next couple of
weeks life certainly wouldn't be dull.

Pulling into her apartment complex, she thought
about Nick and those crazy moments when she'd
first seen him, when her heart had filled so completely with him. The intensity of her reaction had
surprised her. She'd thought that the passing of time,
the living of life over the past year would have dulled
the edges of her feelings for him.

She was disappointed that it hadn't been desire
that had driven him to find her, to see her again, but
rather duty and perhaps some threat the bureau held
over his head.

Certainly the bureau could find plenty in Nick's
background and family history to use against him.
Nick's father, Joey Barnes, had been a powerful
member of an organized crime organization. He and
Nick had become estranged when Nick had decided
not to follow in his father's footsteps.

As far as Nick's family was concerned, he owned
a security business that provided the latest technology in home protection systems. The last Lynn knew,
none of his family was aware he worked for the FBI.

As an operating undercover agent, only his superiors and Lynn had known what he really did for a living.

She shoved thoughts of him away as she got out of her car. She had more important things to think about than a lost love. Grabbing the manila folder Blake had given her, she left her car and hurried to her apartment door.

Monday night she'd be on a plane to Miami. Monday was Labor Day and once she arrived in Miami she'd certainly have her work cut out for her.

She placed the folder on the table, then went to the fridge and grabbed a bottle of water. She'd like a beer, but her head was already spinning and the last thing she needed was alcohol to muddy her brain more.

She had no idea if her request for Nick as a contact would be granted. She'd certainly learned not to believe any promises that were made to her. But, all personal feelings aside, she knew Nick's capabilities, she trusted his intelligence and would feel much better about everything if he was there.

With a sigh she opened the folder and began to study the aerial shots of Stingray Wharf. A year ago when she'd left Miami there had been rumors that the small port would be closed and ships would be routed through the bigger, more up-to-date port of Miami. Apparently that hadn't happened.

Although international traffic was sparse at the small wharf, it was still there.

She sat there for over an hour, studying maps

and reading the information that had been provided for her.

When she felt she'd had enough and couldn't think another minute she closed the file and carried it with her to the spare room. She placed it in a locked file cabinet then sat down at her computer and booted it up.

A glance at her wristwatch let her know it was just after eight. She fought against a wave of exhaustion. Her head felt mired in directions and specs. But, it was too early to go to bed. She'd work for a couple of hours then call it a night.

Thankfully her computer booted up without a problem. Now that she'd agreed to work with the FBI she assumed the little bug they'd planted had been removed.

She thought about running some tests, trying to discern how they had gotten in and what kind of virus they'd planted, but quickly dismissed the idea. Whatever they had done, she knew there would be no trace of it now.

The first thing she did was check her e-mail. There had been a time in her life, when she'd been living with Jonas, when e-mail had been her link to the outside world.

Jonas had raised her to be afraid, to believe that because of his wealth and her special gifts, she could easily become a target of a kidnapper. He'd discouraged her having friends, had been overly protective to a fault. During those years Lynn had found her social time with e-mail and chat rooms.

She frowned as she saw the familiar address of
Delphi@orcl.org.

What now? She opened it and read the message.

Lynn,
Oracle is waiting for you. The Cassandras need you.
For more information contact Kim Valenti at NSA.

There was a phone number included.

The Cassandras. Any trace of sleepiness vanished
as she reread the e-mail. Cassandra, daughter of
Priam and Hecuba, king and queen of Troy in Greek
poetry. The piece of trivia popped into her head, the
result of years of surfing the Internet for entertainment and education.

But, the Cassandras held a more personal
meaning to Lynn. Her mother, Rainy Miller Carrington, and the friends she'd made when she'd been
a student at Athena Academy years ago had called
themselves the Cassandras. Rainy, a senior student
then, had mentored the group of new students, as
was the practice at Athena Academy. Eventually the
motley crew had become best of friends.

Those friends had been responsible for solving
the mystery of Rainy's tragic death in a car accident.
They were also the women Lynn now called friends.

She couldn't leave for Florida without addressing
this new kink. If the Cassandras needed her, then
she'd do whatever she could to help them. Those
same women had gone out of their way to help Lynn

find out about her history. They had risked their careers, their lives to find out the truth about the conspiracy and secrets surrounding Lynn's birth. And they had embraced her as one of their own.

Even though it was Labor Day weekend she picked up her phone and dialed the number listed. It was a Maryland area code.

"Hello?" A woman answered on the first ring.

"I'd like to speak to Kim Valenti," Lynn said. "This is Lynnette White."

"Lynn, I've been waiting for your call. We need to talk. Can we meet?"

"Just tell me where and when," Lynn replied.

"You'll be contacted."

There was a click and Lynn realized she was listening to the faint hum of an empty line. On impulse, she tried to dial back and it rang twice before she got a recording that the number had been disconnected.

She set the phone back in the receiver. What was this, National Conspiracy Week in the United States? First the FBI and now this. Why the need for such subterfuge?

Apparently there was nothing she could do but wait to find out what that was about. She quickly scanned through the rest of her e-mail then shut off the computer. She was still seated at her computer staring at the blank screen thoughtfully when someone knocked.

She cracked the door open an inch to peer outside. Standing there was a delivery guy, a pleasant smile on his youthful face. "Pizza delivery," he said and pulled a flat box from its red insulated carrier.

"But, I didn't..." She bit off her protest that she hadn't ordered a pizza. "What do I owe you?" She opened the door wider.

"It's already taken care of, tip and all." He handed her the warm box. "Enjoy." He turned and hurried back to the car illegally parked against the curb.

Lynn locked the front door, then took the box into the kitchen where she set it on the table and opened it. A pepperoni and mushroom pizza stared back at her and tucked beneath one edge of the crust was a small envelope that was already drawing grease.

She pulled it free and opened it.

Tomorrow night. Six o'clock at Cactus Grill on Scottsdale Road.

The woman she'd spoken to on the phone had said she'd be contacted.

Contact made.

Lynn sank down at the table and pulled a piece of the cheese-laden pizza free. As she took a bite of the pizza she tried to still the feeling that she was in way over her head and this might be her symbolic last supper before her life exploded into something she no longer recognized.

Chapter 4

The rock glistened in the spotlight overhead, its many facets catching the light and sparkling brilliantly as it rested on the black velvet inside the display case.

Her heart banged a frantic rhythm as she slowly descended from the rope that dangled through the skylight directly above the valuable diamond.

She'd already bypassed the security system. All she had to worry about was the very human element of a night guard.

A trickle of perspiration slid down the center of the back of her tight black T-shirt but she was focused only on one thing. Grab the diamond, get the hell out of here and get home. It was what she'd been trained to do.

She paused as she dangled just above the display. Tilting her head to one side she used her acute hearing to listen.

The hum of the air conditioner.

The faint tick of a wall clock from another room.

A whisper of classical music coming from a radio down the hallway in the security guard's room.

Nothing to give her pause.

She inched another foot down the rope, the top of the display case now within the reach of her fingertips. Beautiful. The diamond was so beautiful and within seconds it would be in her hands.

But, of course she wouldn't keep it. She would give it to Uncle Jonas and he would see to it that it was returned to the African government, the rightful owner of the jewel.

She froze.

Was that the sound of breathing? Was she not alone in the room?

"Freeze! FBI."

The glare of bright lights. The click of a safety on a gun. One heartbreaking glimpse of Nick with his gun drawn on her and his face expressing stunned disbelief.

Lynn gasped and sat up with a start. Sweat slicked her skin and the bedsheets held her legs captive in a jumbled mess. Her heart raced as if on the verge of exploding from exertion. She drew a deep breath and untangled herself from the covers.

The faint gray light of predawn filtered in through her bedroom curtains, orienting her to the fact that it had been nothing more than a dream. A dream rooted in memories of the past and what had once been a reality.

Rather than a glittering jewel, she'd been in the process of stealing a precious vase from a museum display when she'd been busted by the FBI. She'd never forget how she felt when she'd seen Nick there and realized the man she'd been sleeping with, the man she knew as head of security for Jonas, was actually an undercover agent.

Learning that Jonas was a criminal had been nothing compared to how betrayed she'd felt by Nick. At that moment she'd believed that all his words of love, his tenderness and passion had been nothing more than an act to gain her confidence.

It was only as they'd worked together to bring down Jonas that she'd come to believe that the love he professed to have for her was real.

She drew a second shuddering breath in an attempt to leave the dream behind.

Jewel thief.

Cat burglar.

That's what she'd been in her previous life. And now the authorities wanted her to use those same skills, enhanced by her special genetic gifts, to advance their own agenda.

During all the daring things she'd done in her past, she'd never truly felt afraid of the consequences. Her lack of fear had partly been because Jonas had convinced her they had the sanctity of the government behind them.

He had told her that if she were caught on one of the nightly forays, the worst that would happen would be that she'd spend a few hours in jail until they could sort it all out and get her released.

She'd been too naive to recognize the real danger she'd been in and so had not suffered any real, bone-chilling fear. But minutes later as she stood beneath the shower, the chill of fear swept through her despite the warmth of the spray of water.

What she was about to do for the FBI was more than a little bit dangerous. There would be real dogs with real teeth, real guards with real guns and perhaps a bomb put together with the express purpose of causing death and destruction.

She'd be a fool not to be afraid.

She dressed in a pair of jeans and a sleeveless light pink blouse then pulled her hair into a ponytail and headed into the kitchen for coffee.

As she drank a cup of the brew, she wondered what the day would bring. Supposedly she would be briefed and trained for the job ahead. And if that wasn't enough to make her nervous, she also had a meeting with a stranger who apparently wanted something from her as well.

Two hours later she drove back to the warehouse

where she would spend the day training for the work at the wharf.

"Good, you're right on time," Blake said when she walked in. "We have a lot of work to do to prepare you before you get on your flight tomorrow night." He ushered her down a long hallway and into a large room that was equipped with floor mats, exercise equipment, ropes and weights. There was also a table and a blackboard at one end of the room.

A tall, thin, gray-haired man entered the room. He had a kind face with brown eyes that exuded warmth. "Lynn, this is Agent William Stewart," Blake said. "He's going to be in charge of giving you a crash course in bomb detection."

"Ms. White." The older man held out a hand. "It's nice to meet you."

"Please, make it Lynn." She took his hand in a firm shake.

"Then call me Bill."

"I'll just let you two get to work," Blake said and without another word he disappeared out the door, leaving Lynn and Bill to begin the day.

By noon Lynn's head was reeling. She'd learned how to use a handheld scanner to detect radioactive material, she'd memorized page after page of material describing the bombs most frequently used by terrorist groups and she'd watched horrifying films of what those bombs were capable of doing to people and property.

"What happens if you're wrong?" she asked Bill

as they ate a sack lunch that had been provided for them. "What happens if your sources are wrong and a bomb isn't coming into Stingray Wharf, but rather another port?"

"Then we hope that the security measures that port has in place picks up on it before it detonates." He paused a moment, then continued. We believe the chatter we've heard concerning Stingray Wharf is reliable. Our sources in this matter have proven to be right many times before. You're faster and more skilled than all of our other agents put together." He smiled sadly then. "It's dangerous times we live in, Lynn. And unfortunately, dangerous times make for desperate men. Because of your special skills, those men believe you're the person for this job. If there is a bomb and if you succeed in finding it before it detonates, you'll be saving hundreds, maybe thousands of lives."

For the first time Lynn recognized the full gravity of what she'd agreed to do, but more, she recognized the grave consequences of what might happen if she didn't succeed.

"Our sources also tell us that you're a pretty amazing woman when it comes to your physical skills."

She shrugged. "I train hard." There was no way she wanted these men to know that her skills came from genetic tampering. If they realized that, she was afraid she and her sisters would end up in some sort of laboratory being studied like rats. She prayed that only a very few people had access to the files recovered when the covert and illegal lab that had created Lynn and her sisters had been destroyed.

After lunch it was more of the same, studying, memorizing and learning more about what was expected of her. A few minutes after five o'clock, Blake told her he'd order in dinner, but Lynn told him not to bother.

"I'll get something to eat on the way home," she said, remembering her meeting at six o'clock. "Besides, I've had enough for today."

Blake frowned, obviously a man who didn't like anyone else calling the shots. "We aren't finished here yet. We still have a lot to do."

"You might not be finished, but I am," she replied firmly. "I'm tired, you've shoved a lot of things into my head today. Now I need to go home and take some time to process it all. I'll be here by seven tomorrow morning and we can start again."

Blake's jaw tightened, but he didn't protest as she picked up her purse and left the building. As she drove away from the warehouse she checked her rearview mirror, making sure she wasn't followed.

She didn't trust any of them. If there was one thing Lynn had learned over the last year and a half of her life, it was that blind trust was incredibly dangerous.

As she headed toward Scottsdale she shifted thoughts, wondering what Kim Valenti wanted from her and what it had to do with the Cassandras? She supposed she could ask Kayla Ryan, who was herself a Cassandra, but if Kayla were involved she'd surely have let Lynn know.

So much had happened in the past forty-eight hours—the stop by the cops, the presence of the FBI, Nick showing up and now this, a cryptic message from a woman she'd never met before. Was it any wonder she felt overloaded?

It was just before six when she pulled up in front of the Cactus Grill on Scottsdale Road. She sat in the parking space for a few minutes, clearing her head of the day's activities and preparing herself for whatever lay ahead.

The sun had not yet begun its slow sink in the west and the heat struck her like a slap in the face as she got out of her car.

The Cactus Grill was nothing more than a glorified sports bar with half a dozen television screens flickering with sports images from different channels. Still, Lynn welcomed the very normalcy of the place and the fact that there were a handful of diners sitting at tables around the room. A public place was smart for a meeting with somebody you didn't know.

For the first time since she'd received the first e-mail from Delphi@orcl.org, a wave of apprehension swept through Lynn. There was no way she could know for sure that she was meeting Kim Valenti from NSA.

The hostess, a pleasant Hispanic woman with beautiful long dark hair, smiled at her. "Good evening. Right this way please."

Lynn followed the woman through the general

dining area and into a small private dining room. "Have a seat. Somebody will be with you momentarily."

She hadn't asked how many were dining, nor had she hesitated in leading Lynn back to this private room. Lynn's apprehension increased. Whoever she was meeting knew what she looked like and must have described her to the hostess.

She sat at the table and tried to still the anxiety swirling in sickening circles in her stomach. Too much. Her life had suddenly become too complicated. She had visions of bombs exploding in her head, the faint stir of regret where Nick was concerned and the uncertainty of what was going to happen in the next few minutes.

Closing her eyes, she drew a deep breath and called on her inner strength. Whatever happened here and in Miami, she would get through it. She had the strength of Rainy Miller Carrington flowing in her veins, the support and love of her sisters and Athena Academy friends.

"Lynnette."

Lynn's eyes popped open to see a slender, dark-haired woman step into the room. She quickly got to her feet. "Kim?"

The woman nodded and held out a hand. "It's nice to finally meet you." Her handshake was firm and confident. She released Lynn's hand then motioned Lynn back into her chair and sank into the seat opposite her at the table.

"Thank you for coming. I apologize for the

secrecy in getting you here. We weren't sure who might be monitoring your e-mail and phone calls."

Probably only the FBI, Lynn thought. They were not only monitoring her calls and e-mail, but had also managed to steal at least her immediate future away from her.

"Do you have some sort of identification?" Lynn asked apologetically. She wasn't about to take anything for granted at this point in her life.

Kim looked at her in surprise, then nodded as if in approval. "Yes, of course." She opened her purse, withdrew a wallet, then pulled out a driver's license and passed it across the table to Lynn.

Lynn studied the license, noting the Maryland address. Kim had come a long way on short notice to meet her. Satisfied that Kim was who she said she was, she returned the identification to her. "Sorry, I just needed to make sure."

Kim smiled. "Please, don't apologize for being smart."

"So, what am I doing here?" Lynn asked, cutting to the chase.

"We'll talk after we're served," Kim replied. "I hope you don't mind, but I took the liberty of ordering for us ahead of time. I wasn't sure what you'd like so I ordered a sampler platter."

The words were barely out of her mouth before the waitress appeared carrying a huge platter. She set the large plate in the center of the table, then placed smaller plates in front of Lynn and Kim. Drinks were served, then the waitress left the small dining room, closing the door behind her.

It wasn't until each of the women had served themselves a portion of the food from the platter that Kim spoke again. "I'm a graduate of Athena Academy. Your mother and her Cassandras were legendary at the school. I didn't know them personally at school—I was younger than them—but I can tell you they were all greatly admired."

"They're wonderful, strong women," Lynn said. "Unfortunately, I never got to know my mother, either."

"But, you've heard the stories. You know how she took a group of girls from diverse backgrounds and got them to pull together as a team the likes of which the Academy has never seen since."

"The Cassandras. Yes, I've heard the stories." They had told Lynn story after story of her mother in an attempt to feed the hunger in Lynn's soul. The remaining Cassandras—Samantha St. John, Tory Patton, Josie Lockworth, Darcy Allen, Kayla Ryan and Alex Forsythe, had adopted Lynn, and her sisters, and through their stories Lynn had learned about the kind of woman her biological mother had been. An accomplished lawyer, a loving wife and a woman who'd given up her life in pursuit of the truth.

Lynn smiled at Kim, noting how the peach-colored blouse the woman wore complemented her olive complexion. "From all the stories I've heard about her, my mother was a pretty amazing woman."

"From everything I've heard about you, *you're* a

pretty amazing woman," Kim replied with a raised dark brow. "Which brings me to the reason we're here." She put down her fork and leaned forward. "We need your help."

"Who is *we*?"

Kim paused a moment to take a sip of her iced tea. When she placed the glass back on the table she looked at Lynn once again, her brown eyes somber. "What I'm about to tell you is top secret. You can't repeat any of the information to another soul. The lives of many people rest on your word that you will keep this in the strictest confidence."

"I understand," Lynn replied. It seemed she'd heard that a lot lately. Don't tell. Strictest confidence. Top secret information.

"You know I'm an NSA code breaker. But I work for a covert organization called Oracle," Kim began. "Oracle is the name of a computer system that was originally designed to track information from the FBI, the CIA and a variety of other intelligence databases. Oracle matches up information that should be shared between the agencies, but often isn't because of territorial shoving matches."

"So, what do you do with this information?" Lynn asked.

"The original purpose was to discover classified information that should be shared between agencies for the best possible effectiveness against enemies of the United States. Even the agencies we monitor don't know we're there."

"Are you Delphi? Is that a code name or something?" Lynn asked, remembering her e-mail had come from Delphi@orcl.com.

"No, I'm not Delphi, and I don't know who is. It is a code name of the person in charge. I told you that secrecy is vital to the agency. I don't know who most of the other Oracle agents are, although the attempt on President Manihon's life last year did bring me into contact with a few, and I don't know who Delphi is. None of the agents do. It's better that way. We're told information on a strictly need-to-know basis."

It was Lynn's turn to take a drink of her iced tea as she tried to process everything that Kim had told her. "So, what do you want from me?"

"We know about your genetic enhancements, but what we really need from you is your amazing computer skills and intelligence. We'd like your help in decoding the Spider files—part of thousands of encrypted files that came into the NSA's possession with the fall of Lab 33."

The mention of Lab 33 sent a wave of bone-chilling coldness through Lynn. Lab 33 had been the secret laboratory responsible for creating her and her sisters. There, in the middle of nowhere in New Mexico, scientists had performed experiments in cloning, mind control hypnosis and a variety of other horrible research that had been outside the realm of any ethics or moral issues.

It had been there that Rainy Miller's stolen eggs

had been genetically altered to produce "super" eggs, eggs that had eventually become Lynn and her two sisters, Dawn and Faith.

"The Spider files?" Lynn eyed Kim curiously. "What exactly are the Spider files?"

"When Lab 33 was brought down, the government authorities found numerous encrypted files. Among them were those called the Spider files. In my spare time, I've managed to decode some of the information, enough to know that they include a list of names. One of those names brought the list to Oracle's attention."

"What name is that?"

"Shannon Conner. Ever heard of her?"

Lynn thought. "Isn't she the reporter who broke the story on the hostages a couple months ago? The ones taken in Berzhaan? I know Tory Patton continued the coverage and was part of rescuing them. Kayla and I talked about it. None of the Cassandras think much of Shannon."

Kim's eyes darkened. "Shannon Conner has the dubious honor of being the only girl ever to be expelled from the Athena Academy. She hated the Cassandras, and while she was at the school she did everything she could to tarnish their good image. When her name showed up in the file, it naturally caught our attention. Through NSA, I'm working on many of the Lab 33 files. But Oracle has a particular interest in these files, and Delphi thinks you're the best person to tackle them. They're low priority for

NSA, and won't be looked at for a while. But they are of special interest to the women of Athena Academy."

As far as Lynn was concerned, Lab 33 was a place of evil and the men who had worked there were responsible for her growing up without knowing her mother and father. And that had only been the beginning of their crimes against her, her sisters and the mother she'd never known.

"Maybe we'd all be better off if those files were never decoded," she said.

A trace of sympathy lit Kim's dark eyes. "I understand how you feel, but, Lynn, whatever information is contained in those files, I can promise you it will only be used for good."

She leaned back in her chair, her gaze still intent on Lynn. "We aren't sure what might be there. We both know how deadly secrets can be and as long as those files remained encrypted and unread, there will forever be a shroud of mystery that remains."

Kim's dark eyes radiated the same kind of strength that Lynn often saw in the eyes of the remaining Cassandras. "This can be your final revenge on Lab 33, revealing the secrets they hoped would never be revealed, shining light on exactly what was happening there."

Lynn could almost feel the warmth of Rainy's love for the child she'd never known letting her know that this was the right thing to do. For Rainy. For the Cassandras. "When do you want me to start?"

"Immediately. The files will be delivered to you

on disk sometime tonight. The sooner you can decode them, the better." Kim stood. "If I need to contact you again, it will be by e-mail. Other than that, we'll have no further contact."

She pulled a slip of paper from her purse. "When you've accomplished the decoding, e-mail Delphi@orcl.com."

"But, I tried to e-mail that address when I got the first message, and my reply bounced back." Lynn said.

Kim smiled. "It will work now. We hope to hear from you soon."

Lynn nodded and thought about mentioning that she would be out of town for a couple of weeks, but realized it didn't matter. She could take her laptop with her and work on the files while she was gone.

She had no idea if anyone from the FBI was somehow monitoring her computer use, but she figured she was as smart as anyone in the employ of that agency when it came to computers. Now that she'd seen what they were capable of, she'd raise her security measures so that the feds monitoring her wouldn't be able to break into the Spider files or see what she was doing with them.

Even though she trusted Kim, it had been pounded into her head all day long that nobody could know about her mission to Miami for the FBI. She had more secrets than a crooked politician.

"Good luck, Lynn. We're depending on you."

Before Lynn had an opportunity to say anything else, Kim Valenti slipped out the door.

It was only at that moment that Lynn realized neither of them had touched the food that had been served.

She looked at the array of appetizers and decided that the discussion of Lab 33 had effectively killed her appetite. She pushed away from the table and stood, amazed by the direction her life was taking her.

She had a bomb to find, secret files to decode and the memory of a lost love to haunt her in whatever quiet moments she might have left in her life.

"Your flight leaves at eight tonight," Blake told Lynn. It was late afternoon and once again she was seated in his office. "That will get you into Miami by one."

The morning and early afternoon had flown by as her training at the warehouse had continued. Bill Stewart and Blake had not only shoved a vast amount of information into her head, but they'd also given her a variety of physical tests to perform, as well.

It had been obvious that they had been both surprised and pleased by the results of those physical tests. But she hadn't even begun to show them what she was capable of.

"This is the address to your new apartment." Blake shoved a piece of paper across the desk. "And this is the key to the apartment. I'll warn you, it's not even close to the Ritz, although we have managed to get Internet access in your unit. It's a small studio and the neighborhood is tough, populated mostly by dockworkers and prostitutes."

Although it certainly didn't sound inviting, she told herself she could endure anything for a week or two. "What's my cover story?"

"Whatever you want to make it. Of course, it's in your best interest to keep to yourself and not invite confidences of any kind with anyone, but if somebody starts asking questions, all they need to know is that you're looking for a new start and this apartment was all you could afford or whatever."

He passed her another set of keys. "These go to your car, which is a ten-year-old black sedan. The license number is BAW029. It will be parked in the lot at your apartment complex, although I doubt you'll need to use it much. The docks are only about six blocks from the apartment building." Lynn took the keys from him, the metal warm in her cold hands.

"And this is your unofficial search warrant." He handed her a velvet pouch.

She knew instantly what the pouch contained. She opened it to look at the lock-picking tools nestled inside. She'd once owned a set very much like this one, bought for her by Jonas.

With these tools she could get through almost any locked door, leaving no trace on the lock that it had been tampered with in any way.

She ran her fingers across several of the tools.

Holding the pouch in her hand made her assignment heart-stoppingly real.

"The best hours for you to conduct your search will be between midnight and three. It is vital that you move as quickly as possible to get to as many containers as you can each evening. The containers of interest will be the ones dropped off each day. We're fairly certain the containers that have been there for days or weeks pose no real threat."

He passed an envelope across the desk. "Here is your airline ticket, a phone contact to be used only in case of the discovery of a bomb and enough cash to take care of your living expenses while you're working with us."

Lynn took the envelope and felt the heft of the cash bulging the seams. At least she wouldn't starve while working for the FBI.

"If anything changes you'll be contacted through e-mail, however you will not be able to contact us through that avenue. I guess that's it. I'd better let you get out of here so you can pack and prepare for your trip." Blake rose from his chair and Lynn did the same.

She was already packed. When she'd gotten home from the Cactus Grill the night before, she'd spent the next hour packing her suitcase and laptop for her trip.

When she'd finished she'd sat in a chair in her living room, waiting for the Spider files to be delivered. At midnight there had been a sharp knock on her door. When she'd answered she'd found a small package on her doorstep and inside that package had been several disks.

Her first instinct had been to get to work on them, but knowing she had to be here at the warehouse by seven, she'd packed the files in her suitcase and had gone to bed.

"I wish you success, Lynnette," Blake now said and held out his hand to her. "We appreciate you heeding the call of duty."

She eyed him askance. As if she'd had a choice in the matter. "I'll do the best that I can," she said as she shook his hand.

As she left his office, Bill Stewart approached her. "All set?" he asked.

She smiled at him. Over the course of the last forty-eight hours she'd come to like the agent, with his warm brown eyes and friendly smile. "I guess I'm as set as I'm going to get."

"Come on, I'll walk you out to your car."

He fell in step with her as they walked back through the warehouse. "Is this all set up for the Stingray Wharf thing?" she asked, gesturing to the men at work at their phones and computers.

"No, this base of operations was set up to deal with something else here in Arizona," Bill said. "It has nothing to do with the terrorist threat in Miami."

"How long have you been an FBI agent?" Lynn asked as they stepped out into the late-afternoon heat.

"I've been with the Bureau for over twenty years, but I've only been working with this particular group a little over a year."

"And what is the name of this particular group?" So, Nick had been correct, the men she would be working for were some sort of splinter under the guise of the FBI.

"If I told you that, I'd have to kill you." Although his tone was light and teasing, Lynn knew he wasn't going to tell her anything more about the men or the specific organization he currently worked with.

She was on a need-to-know basis only and apparently they didn't think she needed to know anything more than what she'd been told.

They reached her car and she opened the driver's side door to allow it to air out a minute before getting inside the hot interior. "Thanks for everything, Bill. You're a good teacher."

He smiled. "A good student makes it easy to be a good teacher." His smile faded as he held out his hand to her. "Good luck, Lynn." He grabbed her hand in a firm shake. His warm brown eyes held a trace of sadness as he released her hand. "I hope someday we meet again."

He didn't wait for her reply, but instead turned crisply on his heel and strode back toward the warehouse, his silver hair shining in the waning light.

Lynn stared after him. There had been something in his eyes that made her think he didn't believe they would ever meet again. Something in the dark depths that had made her believe Agent William Stewart didn't think she would survive this assignment.

Chapter 5

The flight touched down in Miami at a few minutes after midnight East Coast time. It was after twelve-thirty by the time Lynn got off the plane, retrieved her suitcase from the luggage carousel and hailed a cab to take her to her new, temporary life.

The scents and the sights as the cab drove her toward the Stingray Wharf area were achingly familiar and brought back memories of her former life here in Miami.

Before she'd discovered that she was nothing more than a pawn in Jonas's illegal activities, she'd had a life most would have envied. She'd had the best of everything, but had also suffered a depth of loneliness that few people would understand.

Nick had understood.

She couldn't revisit those memories without thinking of Nick and the passion and caring they'd found together. She'd never be able to think of him without wondering what would have happened had she stayed in Miami.

Would their love have continued to grow and flourish or would they have discovered that it had been emotion born from circumstance and nothing more than a brief illusion?

She'd wondered often about her feelings for Nick in those first months of living in Phoenix. She'd wondered if maybe she'd felt so intensely for him simply because he'd been at the right place at the right time. Could he have been any man who paid attention to her?

Loneliness had been the only constant companion in her life, and she'd been hungry for male attention. Was it any wonder that she'd thrived beneath Nick's heated gazes and sweet touch?

She was the first to admit that she was no longer that hungry, lonely young woman she'd been. She'd changed and there was no way of knowing how much Nick had changed in the time they'd been apart.

"You sure this is the address you want?" the cabby asked from the front seat. He adjusted the rearview mirror so his gaze met hers.

Lynn leaned forward. "Positive. Why? Is there a problem?"

"No, no problem. It's just kind of a rough area for a young woman."

"Yeah well, what are you going to do? It's home for now." She leaned back in the seat and redirected her attention out the window.

The streets they were traveling now were a long way from the streets Lynn had known when she'd lived here. Then, she'd known where to find all the most expensive boutiques, the finest dining establishments and upscale spas and clubs.

Then, it had been nothing for her to spend on a pair of shoes what she now paid in rent for her apartment in Phoenix. The tips she'd left at restaurants now paid for weekly groceries. Still, she didn't miss her old life. She preferred having less and being her own person.

These streets were dark, with broken streetlights and boarded-up buildings. At this time of night few people were out, and those who were clung to the shadows, never fully revealing themselves.

She leaned her head back against the seat and closed her eyes. Would Nick be her contact here in Miami? She knew that just because she'd requested him didn't mean that he'd be the agent assigned to this particular job.

Her feelings about working with him again were mixed. The moment she'd seen him again all the old feelings had rushed in and she'd felt a happiness she hadn't known since the last time she'd seen him.

But those feelings had been tempered by the fact that he hadn't sought her out because he couldn't live without her, hadn't hunted her down because he needed to see her, he'd simply been doing what he'd been commanded to do.

Thoughts of Nick fled as the cabby came to a halt in front of a three-story brick apartment building. Even though Blake had warned her that it was a tough area and her expectations for her living arrangements had been low, this place was more dismal than she'd anticipated.

She stepped out of the backseat of the cab and the first thing that struck her was the smell. The scents of briny salt and rotting fish mingled with oil and gasoline to produce a distinctly unpleasant odor. Trash spilled out of cans that lined the sidewalk, the acrid smell only adding to the repellent mix.

As the cabby pulled her large suitcase from his trunk, Lynn scanned the surrounding area. At the nearest intersection the streetlight was dark, but beer signs from a tavern illuminated a handful of big, burly men standing on the corner. Raucous jukebox music poured from the open door of the bar.

Across the street a lone woman stood in a sparkly miniskirt that bared long, bony legs and a blouse that barely hid the biggest breasts Lynn had ever seen. As she paid the cabby she felt the malevolent glare from the woman following her every movement.

Lynn grabbed her suitcase and large briefcase

and headed into the building. The lobby was nothing more than a small enclosure containing a single elevator. The pungent smell of stale cooking odors, urine and body perspiration caused Lynn's nose to wrinkle in defense. It was the smell of hopelessness and despair, of shattered lives and misery.

A week, two at the most, she told herself as she stepped into the elevator that would take her to her apartment on the third floor.

Thankfully she encountered nobody on her way to apartment 306. She steeled herself as she opened the door and flipped on the light switch to give her a first glimpse of the place she would call home.

It was bad, but it wasn't as bad as she'd expected after walking through the lobby. As Blake had said, it was a studio with a kitchenette against one wall. The kitchen appliances were avocado green, definitely antiques, as were the rest of the sparse furnishings, but at least it looked clean and the door had both a chain and a dead bolt to assure security while she was inside.

She dropped her suitcase and briefcase to the floor and took a moment to explore. A tiny closet would hold what few clothes she'd brought and the bathroom had a stand-up shower, but no tub.

She assumed the new shiny phone outlet near the kitchen table would provide Internet access and she quickly set up her computer there.

It took her less than half an hour to finish unpacking, then she went to the single window the apartment boasted and opened the blinds to stare out into the night.

From this vantage point she could not only see the bar on the corner but could also hear the music that poured out of the establishment.

If she focused her hearing she knew she'd be able to distinguish the deep voices of the men standing in front of the door of the place, even hear the clink of glasses from inside and the brush of jean-clad legs as people walked in and out.

She'd learned as a young child how to tune out the sounds that created a mindless cacophony in her head due to her acute hearing abilities. It had been a skill of survival.

She closed the blinds and rubbed eyes that felt gritty from exhaustion. She'd hoped to catch a little sleep on the plane, but a squalling, kicking toddler in the seat directly behind her had made that impossible.

A sudden thought struck her. She'd left Phoenix without telling anyone where she was going or how long she'd be gone. If something happened to her here, she didn't trust the authorities to see to it that any of her friends or any of her family heard about it.

On impulse she got up and dug her cell phone out of her purse, then punched in the numbers that would connect her to her sister, Faith.

As she waited for Faith to answer, she walked back to the window and stared out at the dismal sur-roundings. Several motorcycles were now parked in front of the bar and the group of men milling about had grown. Through the glass of the window she could hear their voices talking and laughing with each other.

"Lynn?" Her sister's voice sounded sleepy. It must be after midnight in New Orleans.

"Hi, sis." Lynn moved away from the window and returned to the sofa. "I know it's late but I just felt like it was time for a quick check-in. How are you?"

"Where are you?" Faith demanded.

"I took a couple of weeks off and decided to visit Miami," Lynn said.

There was a long pause. "Are you in trouble, Lynn?"

There were times when Lynn thought it was cool to have a sister who had psychic abilities, but it sucked when she had secrets she didn't want her sister to know.

"No, it's nothing like that," Lynn replied and hoped she convinced Faith. "I just got a little homesick for Miami. So, how is Roy? You two still an item?" It was a conscious effort on Lynn's part to change the subject.

"As far as I'm concerned he's still the hottest detective in the world. He makes me happy, Lynn. What about you? Have you finally taken pity on that lovesick neighbor of yours?"

Lynn laughed and easily imagined her sister with her golden blond hair and eyes that looked so much like Lynn's own. "No, and don't hold your breath where Leo is concerned."

There was another long pause. "You sure you're all right, Lynn? I'm definitely picking up some strange vibes from you."

"Maybe you're just suffering a little indigestion," Lynn replied with forced lightness. The last thing she wanted was for Faith to worry about her. She had enough to worry about working with the police and using her psychic abilities to help crack difficult cases. "I'm fine, really. I just got in and if you hear anything in my voice, it's probably nothing more than exhaustion."

"Then get to bed," Faith said sternly. "And call me tomorrow." She paused a long moment. "Lynn, does this trip to Miami have anything to do with a certain man?"

"I don't know…maybe." It was far easier to let Faith think that this trip to Miami was motivated by a man. Faith knew all about Lynn's past relationship with Nick.

"Unfinished business," Faith said. "You two never really had a definitive end to things. Just don't get hurt, Lynnie."

"Believe me, that's the last thing I want to happen."

The sisters said their goodbyes, then Lynn hung up. She shook her head ruefully. She should have known better than to call Faith. When she'd felt the need to connect with somebody, she should have called Dawn. At least Dawnie didn't have psychic abilities.

But, Dawn was currently off on an adventure—

Dawn-speak for dangerous covert mission—in Europe with the man in her life, Des Asher. It was always more difficult to get hold of Dawn than it was to connect by phone with Faith.

Bone weary, she sank down on the threadbare sofa-sleeper, trying to decide if she wanted to make it into a bed or just crash on it in sofa form.

Her eyes grew heavy and she was almost asleep when she heard the faint sound of knuckles rapping on her door. She shot up like a cow poked with a cattle prod, adrenaline spiking through her.

Who was at her door? How many of those rough-looking men on the corner might have seen her arrive, a slender young woman all alone? It was possible that one of them had seen her as an opportunity, an easy mark to exploit.

She moved to the door and strained to hear any sound from the other side. Nothing. Making certain the chain was firmly fastened, she unlocked the dead bolt and eased the door open just a fraction of an inch, just enough to peer out and see Nick.

She quickly unfastened the chain and opened the door.

"Nice place," he said dryly as he swept past her.

"I can't say I'm overly thrilled with my new address," she replied as she refastened the locks then turned to face him.

There was no denying it. She was glad to see him. "I'm assuming you're going to be my contact?" she asked, needing to confirm what she hoped was the truth.

"That's what I was told as of this morning." His jaw knotted with tension. He placed a small black duffel bag on top of the table next to her computer.

Did he hate the idea of working with her again? Was he harboring a grudge because she'd left Miami, left him and things between them had fallen apart? Or did he just not care? Had he never really cared?

Business. She had to focus on business.

"I wanted to make sure you'd gotten in okay and go over things with you before you officially start tomorrow night," he said.

She nodded and there was a long moment of awkward silence. "I'd offer you something to drink but the cupboards are bare," she said as he sat at the small kitchenette table and gestured her into the chair opposite him.

Once again she noticed the changes in him. When he'd worked for Jonas, he'd always been impeccably dressed and groomed. He'd looked smooth and debonair.

Now, with his hair in need of a good cut and his jaw shadowed with a five o'clock beard, clad in worn jeans and a T-shirt advertising Harley Hogs, he looked as if he belonged on the mean streets outside. She even thought she smelled the faint aroma of cigarette smoke clinging to him.

A chameleon. The man had the capacity to blend into any crowd, walk any street and look as if he belonged. She had a feeling it was part of what made him so good at undercover work. And even though he could use a shave and a haircut, there was no denying that he looked hot.

"I'm glad to see you. I'm glad you're going to be my contact. You look well, Nick," she said, unable to stop herself.

He grinned, that slow sexy smile that she remembered from the past, had cherished in her dreams. "Thanks, but I know I look like hell," he replied. His gaze swept the length of her and she was glad she'd decided to wear the forest-green dress that pulled the green from her eyes and complemented her chestnut hair. "You, on the other hand, look amazing."

For just a moment as his warm gaze caressed her, it felt as if no time had passed between them, no distance had ever occurred. The awkwardness fell away and her heart stuttered in that old familiar way as her breath caught deep in her chest.

There was a light in his eyes that made her believe he felt it, too, the spark, the magic that had once existed between them, that still existed and just waited for a breath of air to ignite it into a full-blown fire once again.

He cleared his throat and broke the moment by averting his gaze from her and to the bag on the table in front of him. "I brought you some surprises." He opened the zipper on the bag.

"I don't suppose there's a cold beer in there?" she said, trying to keep the tone light and easy.

He quirked a dark eyebrow. "Afraid not." Once again his long-lashed dark brown eyes met hers. "But, maybe when this is all over we can have a few cold brews together."

"I'd like that." And more, she thought. "So, what have you brought me?"

"A pretty pin for your blouse that is actually a transmitter. I want you to wear it to the dockyard each night. That way I'll be able to hear everything that's going on and will know if you get into trouble."

"And what happens if I get caught and the authorities find the transmitter? How will I explain that away if according to the FBI I'm a lone wolf who's gone back to my criminal ways?" She couldn't keep a trace of bitterness from her voice.

"If you get caught, you lose it. I've seen you move, Lynn. I know you can yank that thing off and toss it away in the blink of a man's eye." He frowned, and once again his jaw tensed into a knot. "Look, I don't like what the Feds are doing with you any more than you do. If I had my way I wouldn't have anything to do with this entire operation."

"So, why are you here now? I mean, you did what they requested of you—you convinced me that I had no alternative but to work for them."

"I'm here partly because you requested me and partly because I don't trust anyone else to be as careful as I'll be to keep you safe."

His words warmed her, but she wasn't about to get all gushy and silly.

The sight of him might cause her heart to beat a little faster, her memories of him could stir her on one level, but despite his words she still felt an emotional distance radiating from him that kept those old feelings in check.

"I asked for you because you're the only agent I felt I could trust to watch my back. I don't trust any of those other bastards." Although William Stewart hadn't been bad.

Again that charming smile curved his lips. "Welcome to my world."

"It's a hell of a way to live," she replied.

He nodded. "I told you the other night, the men in charge of this particular operation aren't the kind of FBI men I usually work for. They play hardball like nobody I've ever worked with before."

"You've got that right," she replied. "What else do you have in that bag of tricks?"

He reached inside the duffel bag. "A handheld radiation scanner." He pulled the piece of equipment out and laid it on the table between them. "I was told you knew how to use it."

She nodded. "Part of my training before I left Phoenix."

"My last surprise for you is a prepaid phone, a throwaway. It's programmed to speed dial another prepaid phone, one that I have in my pocket. It's for emergency use only."

He placed the phone on the table and once again eyed her intently. "I'm sure they told you how dangerous this is."

"They did."

Raking a hand through his hair, he stood and walked over to the window. He flipped open the blinds and stared out, not speaking for several minutes.

She watched him as he stood motionless, noting the breadth of his shoulders, his slim hips and long legs. He wore a pair of jeans better than any man she'd ever known.

He turned to face her once again and his eyes were dark, his expression enigmatic. "I can only give you three hours a night, Lynn. I've got something else going on that requires the rest of my time. That means for twenty-one hours a day you're on your own in this ungodly neighborhood."

"I'm a big girl. I know how to take care of myself."

"You'll have to." He looked at his watch and frowned. "I need to go now, but I'll be back here tomorrow night by midnight."

She got up from the table and walked the short distance with him to her door. She unfastened the chain and twisted the dead bolt, then turned back to face him.

"Thank you, Nick. Thank you for working this with me."

He raised a hand, as if to touch her face, but

quickly dropped it to his side. "It's the least I can do considering I was partially responsible for getting you into this mess."

"I know how these people work, I know you didn't have any choice in coming to talk to me. No hard feelings."

He cocked his head to one side. "No hard feelings about anything?"

Suddenly their past came between them. It begged to be addressed, needed to be somehow resolved. "Why would I have hard feelings about anything? I was the one who left, Nick. I was the one who left you and Miami behind."

This time when he raised his hand it was to lightly touch her face. His fingertips were warm as they trailed down her cheek to her jaw, then fell away. "You had to go. There were things you needed to do, things you needed to find out." His gaze was as warm as his fingers and in the depths of them Lynn saw a whisper of desire. It was there only a moment, then gone.

He jammed his hands into his pockets. "It's over and done. We can't let the past interfere with our job. Things are different now, we're different." He checked his watch once again and frowned. "I really need to get out of here. I'll see you tomorrow night at midnight."

The minute he slid out the door, Lynn once again locked it up tight, then leaned against it and drew in a deep breath. A sense of disturbing disquiet swept through her.

He'd said and done all the right things. But, what bothered her was that the only man she trusted, the "partner" who professed he'd have her back, had dark secrets in his eyes, secrets that made her worry that ultimately she could trust nobody but herself.

As Nick left the apartment building his gaze shot first left, then right, making sure that nobody looking for trouble was nearby. At least his car was still parked where he'd left it. In this kind of neighborhood you never knew what to expect.

He slid behind the steering wheel, locked his doors, then leaned his head back against the seat and wondered how in the hell he was going to survive the next couple of weeks.

It was unprecedented that an agent would work two undercover assignments at the same time. This was the biggest risk Nick had ever taken and in his years of working for the bureau he'd taken plenty of risks.

He dragged a hand down his lower jaw, sat up straight and started the engine. He was exhausted and knew that state was only going to get worse. He had the undercover job he was working in Raymore and now the added stress of being here for Lynn three hours a night.

But he couldn't not be here for Lynn. When he'd heard she'd requested him, had been told what they were asking of her, he'd wanted to be here for her.

Nick had enjoyed the company of many women

in his thirty years of life, but none of them had affected him as deeply, as profoundly as Lynn.

She was the one he'd been unable to forget, the only one who haunted him with thoughts of what might have been. He'd come along in her life at a time when she'd needed things he couldn't offer her. She'd needed to discover who she was, where she'd come from, and to rebuild a life destroyed by lies.

Seeing her again had stirred up old desires, had fired up new wants. He'd thought he'd put her behind him, but the minute he'd laid eyes on her he'd realized she'd never really been out of his heart.

She'd looked dynamite in that sexy green dress and he'd been struck by the desire to unfasten the little buttons that had run down the front, slide it off her shoulders and take his pleasure in kissing each and every inch of exposed skin.

But the timing for their relationship the first time around had been all wrong, and it was even worse now.

He pulled away from the curb and headed back to his life in Raymore, a small town less than an hour away.

If he survived his assignment in Raymore he intended to take time off, reassess what he wanted to do with the rest of his life. He'd been undercover on one assignment or another for the past seven years. He was tired of living lies and moving in the shadows. When this was all over he wanted to find a life that was truly his, one that required no lies and no secrets.

But, in order to accomplish that, he had to survive both the undercover work in Raymore and this new assignment working with Lynn. He couldn't tell her about the Raymore job, couldn't risk her having information that would not only put his own life at risk, but the lives of other agents working there.

This particular operation was the most elaborate Nick had ever been involved in and nothing could jeopardize the efforts to bring down a major drug operation. The complicated scheme had required Nick to make a personal sacrifice, one that would keep him from acting on any desire he might feel for Lynn.

He'd already gone against orders where she was concerned by giving her the prepaid cell phone. He'd been ordered to work with her only as a contact, to not interfere in any way, ride to the rescue or have contact with her outside of the three hours a night.

If the men in charge knew he'd given her a cell phone where he could reach her, he'd be yanked off the case and eventually find himself working a detail in some Podunk town in the middle of nowhere.

The men who'd made the rules wanted her flying solo so that if she fell nothing could be traced back to them. They were covering their asses at the expense of her safety.

What bothered him was that Raymore wasn't that far away from Miami and this part of the city wasn't unfamiliar to the men who marketed the drugs that the operation in Raymore produced.

If there was any bleed over from one assignment to the other, it could spell not only his own death, but Lynn's death, as well.

Chapter 6

Lynn's hands trembled as she pulled up the black Lycra leggings that fit her like a second skin. It had been a long time since she'd worn the tight pants and matching hoodie with the pouch in the front.

They were clothes designed for a thief, black as the shadows of the night and tight enough that no material could be grabbed to hinder escape or restrict her movements.

When she was dressed, she pulled her hair back in a tight ponytail and stared at her reflection in the wavy, dull mirror above the cracked bathroom sink.

Her face was as pale as she'd ever seen it. Her eyes, more gold than green tonight, were unusually wide.

Fear. That's what shone from her eyes. It etched through her and she embraced it, knowing that it was a healthy response to what she was about to do.

It was fear that would keep her cautious.

It was fear that would keep her alive.

She left the bathroom and checked her wrist-watch. Just after eleven. She grabbed a can of diet soda from the refrigerator and cracked it open.

She'd found a deli and grocery store in the next block that morning and had bought enough supplies to get her through the next couple of days. It had only taken one foray outside the apartment to realize it wasn't something she wanted to do often.

Even during the daylight hours the streets were filled with tough-looking men and women, people who weren't the type to shy away from trouble or confrontation. Lynn wasn't looking for trouble and she had no desire to tangle with the locals.

She'd managed to get her groceries and get back inside the apartment without meeting anyone's direct gaze or stirring somebody's irrational ire.

She'd passed the afternoon hours sitting at her computer and beginning the arduous task of trying to decode the Spider files.

Parts of the files were what Kim had already decoded, and what Lynn had discovered had been a list of names of intriguing, world-renowned people, names she'd read about in the news and heard on television. Power players, movers and shakers, and many of them had suffered some sort of scandal or another in the recent past.

It was easy to see why Oracle wanted the rest of the files decoded. She was sure they were looking for some sort of explanation about the list of names, plus a connection to Athena Academy. Unfortunately, the same code that had worked to untangle the first list of encrypted names didn't work on the rest of the file.

When Lynn had been a college student in Miami she'd studied computer science and had been particularly interested in codes and ciphers. She'd developed several programs whose specific functions were decoding and deciphering.

She'd run the first program, which looked for plain text hidden in numerical code. It had been both time-consuming and frustrating as the program had come up with nothing.

Of course, if it had been that easy, Oracle wouldn't have needed to contact her. Numerical codes were some of the easiest to break and almost any adequate cryptologist would have been able to do the job. Lynn felt proud that one as talented as Kim Valenti had trusted her with the job.

She'd worked the computer until dinnertime, then had packed away the Spider files in the bottom of the small closet and had fixed herself some supper.

"You got through the day, now all you have to do is get through the hours of the night," she muttered aloud as she walked to the window and peered outside.

Nick should be arriving before too long, then it would be showtime. She'd be in a shipyard looking for a bomb with no safety net beneath her.

As she waited for Nick she went over everything in her head. According to the paperwork Richard Blake had given her the holding yard closed at 10:00 p.m. After that nobody was allowed in or out. There were usually no less than six armed guards on duty and an equal number of dogs that patrolled the area.

The shipping containers were in rows, stacked two to three high and each numbered so they could be found easily when a truck arrived to carry one away. Because Stingray Wharf was small, the number of containers that arrived each day varied from ten to thirty.

She'd have three hours a night to get through them all. She leaned her forehead against the warm glass of the window. She'd been a pawn in her god-father's life and she was once again a pawn to powers bigger than her own.

In a chess game, pawns were usually sacrificed to protect the queen and she knew that's why the government was using her, because she could be easily sacrificed for their greater good.

It was exactly eleven-forty when a soft knock fell on her door. She opened it to allow in Nick. He gave her a terse nod as he swept through the door, bringing with him the scent of the night.

"I see you survived the day," he said and went

right to the table where she had laid out the items he'd brought with him the night before. He once again had his duffel with him and pulled out a small speaker box.

"I told you I'd be fine. Nobody bothered me all day long."

"Let's hope nobody bothers you all night long, as well. I've got the latest aerial shot of the shipyard," he said and pulled a sheet of paper from the bag. He laid it on the table and Lynn moved closer to look at it.

"These are the containers that were unloaded today. There's a total of thirteen and they were taken to the north side of the lot." His finger pointed to the appropriate area. "These are the ones that need to be checked tonight. As you know, each of them is numbered. When a container is cleared, you need to let me know what the number is so I can put it on a list I'm keeping."

"An inside source?" she asked as she studied the map.

"Apparently." He picked up the tiny transmitter and motioned her to step closer to him. "Any layman who sees this will think it's nothing more than a pretty little lapel pin."

She stood perfectly still as he attached the transmitter on her shirt collar. His familiar scent filled her nose and he was so close to her she could feel the heat from his body warming the air around them.

"With this little thing I'll be able to hear everything you say and some of what is happening around you, but I won't be able to communicate with you," he said when he was finished fastening the little bug to her.

She knew she should step away from him, wondered why he didn't step away from her. But, they remained face-to-face, toe-to-toe and Lynn's breath became labored as their gazes locked.

He frowned. "Lynn, I just want you to know, I thought about you often over the last year." His eyes were as dark as the night outside the window, but lit with a small silver flame in the very center.

His words made her heart swell. "I thought about you, too."

"Before you go, I want to make sure you understand that what I felt for you a year ago was real, that it was never just about doing a job." His frown deepened and he took a step back from her. "I wanted you to know that." He looked at his watch. "And now it's time for you to get out of here."

Although she would have loved to stay and listen to him talk some more, it was time for her to get to the job she'd been sent to do.

She picked up the prepaid phone and stuck it in a pouch in the front of the hoodie where it could rest next to the lock-picking kit, then she grabbed the handheld scanner that would aid her in locating a bomb.

He turned on the speaker box. "Say something so I can test the transmitter."

"Testing...testing." Her voice came out of the speaker.

"Okay. You're good to go," he said. He sat at the table and gazed up at her. "You know if you get into trouble I'm under strict orders not to intervene. I won't be able to help you in any way."

"I figured as much," she replied and walked to the door, her heart beginning a quickened pace as adrenaline swooped through her.

"Lynn, be careful. I want you back here safe and sound."

She flashed him a quick smile. "Believe me, I want the same thing." With those final words, she left the relative safety of her apartment.

The bar was hopping despite the fact that it was almost midnight on a Tuesday night. The strains of "Born To Be Wild" drifted out into the street, accompanied by the sounds of laughter.

The hooker she had seen on the opposite corner the night before wasn't there tonight. That was fine with Lynn. The woman had looked at her as if she'd like nothing more than to stick a knife in her back.

The apartment was six long blocks from the shipyards. Lynn took off running and with each step her heart pumped faster and harder.

Running was one thing she did very well. The genetic enhancements that had been done to her had made her legs faster, stronger than normal human being's.

Too bad those enhancements hadn't managed to make her a heart that didn't respond to fear. But, at the moment her heart banged like a timpani orchestra as fear welled up inside her, fear mixed with a high kick of adrenaline.

She could die tonight. The reality of the potential for imminent death couldn't be denied.

As she drew closer to the yards, she could hear the sounds of the water lapping the shore, striking the sides of ships that were docked. The smell of rotting fish increased as she raced forward, at the same time shunning streetlights and trying to cloak herself in the shadows of the night.

The hood of her lightweight sweatshirt was up around her head, hiding her hair from view. If anything happened she didn't want anyone to be able to identify her.

When she reached the corner directly across from the shipyard's entry, she paused to catch her breath. She leaned against a building and tried to orient herself as to where she needed to go next.

"Nick? I hope you can hear this," she said softly. "I'm directly across from the entry of the yards." She frowned and studied the area. "I think the holding yard is to the right. I'm going to find a place to get inside."

It was relatively easy to get into the shipyard itself. Only a chain-link fence separated the yard from the public area and the public access of the docks was never closed.

She didn't go in through the gate, but instead easily jumped the fence and went down into a crouch, checking for any kind of watchman in the area. Security wouldn't be as tight here. Night traffic would be minimal, but there were still sounds of activity around her.

It would be easier on her if she could just walk through the area and not draw attention to herself, but that wasn't possible. The night was hot and she was dressed inappropriately in the all-black, tight clothing. That alone would draw too much attention and suspicion.

She kept to the shadows, moving in a crouch as she made her way toward the holding area. Within minutes she saw the walls of the enclosure. Ten-foot-high concrete walls offered not only security from any person attempting to get in, but also effective protection from hurricane winds and unusually high surf.

A single entry gate broke the long expanse of concrete. Next to the entry a uniformed guard leaned against the wall, looking bored and half-asleep.

Good. She wanted him to keep looking bored. She checked her wristwatch, where the faintly illuminated dial read exactly midnight.

Time to get to work.

Moving stealthily, she made her way farther from the entry until she reached a corner of the concrete enclosure where the darkness seemed more complete.

For most people a ten-foot concrete wall would be impossible to scale without some kind of tools or at the very least a ladder of sorts. But the height of the wall didn't daunt her.

She stuffed the scanner in her pouch, then bent down and gathered the strength in her legs, knowing that the one thing she could thank Lab 33 for was the genetic enhancements that had been made to give her superstrength and agility.

In one smooth jump, her fingers gripped the edge of the top of the concrete. She hung for a moment, the gritty concrete rough to the point of almost painful beneath her fingertips.

Shoulder joints burning, she drew a deep breath and pulled herself up and over to the other side. She hit the ground with barely a sound and remained perfectly still as she cocked her head and listened.

No sound of running footsteps.

No warning growl from a dog.

No outcry of any kind to indicate that she was busted.

The only sound she could hear was the frantic beat of her own heart. Could Nick hear it? The frenetic pounding of fear? She had no idea how sensitive the little transmitter she wore was.

"I'm in," she whispered.

Aware of minutes ticking by, she headed for the north side of the lot, carefully moving between the rows of containers and praying she encountered nothing else that breathed.

The entire area was concrete and she made sure she moved quietly enough that her sneakers wouldn't make a sound against the surface.

The containers were a variety of sizes, from those

that would fit neatly on the back of a semitrailer to smaller units no bigger than a garden shed.

Hearing still attuned to her surroundings, she crept to the container farthest away from the corner where she'd made entry. She'd start there and work forward.

She pulled a small penlight from her bra and gave a quick shine on the end of the container. A simple padlock secured the door. She pulled out her lock-picking kit and removed the tool to use to breach the lock.

"Yo!" A male voice rode the air, coming from someplace on her right. She flattened herself against the side of the container, praying that she was not visible in the darkness. Had her quick shine of the penlight alerted somebody?

"Yo, yourself," a different male voice replied.

Too close. The voices were far too close for comfort. She remained frozen, scarcely breathing.

"We playing cards tonight?" the first voice asked.

There was an answering deep chuckle. "Is that what you call it? I call it taking your money as easy as taking candy from a baby."

"You funny man, seems I recall last week I relieved you of forty bucks."

"Yeah and the wife bitched about it like I'd lost a hundred."

As the two men talked about their last couple of poker games, Lynn remained deathly still, hoping, praying they finished their conversation quickly and moved to another area of the yard.

Go away, she mentally willed as a trickle of perspiration slid from her hairline and down the side of her face. The two men were in the row next to where she hid. She was aware of the time ticking by, precious time she needed to do her work for the night.

She breathed shallowly through her mouth as she waited. What if they never moved? What if they spent the rest of the night standing there and mouthing about poker games and ex-wives and the problems with their children?

What if she had to remain where she was, plastered against the side of the container until the sun came up and she was discovered?

No, she'd be discovered long before sunrise. At three-thirty there was a shift change and the guards coming on duty at that time would do a sweep of the yard. That's when she'd be found.

If they didn't shoot first and ask questions later, she could look forward to an eight-by-ten cell for many years to come. There would be no more Web site building, no more pizza with Leo and no hope for any kind of a renewed relationship with Nick.

The thought surprised her, but she realized it had always been in her mind. The moment she'd seen Nick she'd wondered if perhaps they'd be able to not renew their old relationship, but build a new one that was even stronger, more enduring than the one they'd had in the past.

She had no idea if it was even possible. She had

no idea if in the year they had been apart he had found somebody else, had a new woman in his life.

Thoughts of Nick vanished as the men's voices moved away. She waited until they were so far in the distance she knew she was safe, then she turned to the padlock and got to work.

Despite the trembling of her fingers it took her only a minute to get the door unlocked and ease it open. Inside she found furniture imported from Indonesia. According to the packing slip, there were twenty-four chairs, three dining tables and ten coffee tables destined for a furniture store in Texas.

She ran the scanner over everything and when it registered nothing, she quickly exited the container and refastened the padlock.

One down. Twelve to go.

Nick stood at the window and waited to hear Lynn's voice come out of the small speaker on the table. He couldn't remember the last time his stomach had been so cramped with nerves. It would have been far easier on him had he been the one in the line of fire.

But, if he'd learned anything about Lynnette White a year ago it was that she wasn't the type to stand back and let a man protect her from whatever danger lay ahead.

When they had taken down her godfather, she had been the one who had demanded a face-to-face meeting with him at Nick's beach cottage. She had been the one who had insisted she be a part of the sting operation to get him behind bars.

She had been strong and commanding that day, showing him new depths of inner strength. It had been her naivete and innocence that had first called him to her, but her strength had made him fall in love with her.

But, that strength was also what had gotten her into the position she now found herself in, working a dangerous job for men who might possibly be equally as dangerous.

She'd been gone a little over two hours and so far had cleared seven containers. Each time there was silence coming from the speaker, Nick's tension twisted tighter in his gut.

"Container 57321 cleared," her voice whispered through the speaker.

He left the window and went back to the table and marked the container on a spreadsheet. Good, that left only five more containers for her to get through then her work for the night would be finished.

He wouldn't relax until she walked unscathed back through the apartment door. Even then his relief would be short-lived. They had a week or two of doing this all over again night after night.

Then, when he left here, he would return to a life of lies and danger, a place where one false move could see his throat slit or a bullet through his brain.

One moment at a time, he told himself. That's the

way he'd been living his life, one moment at a time. He sat at the table and rubbed the back of his neck where a tension headache tried to gain control.

He had no idea how long the operation in Raymore would take place. So far he'd seen the warehouse where the stuff was cooked, he'd watched the meth being packaged and distributed for sale, but the FBI wasn't interested in the mules of the operation.

They wanted the money man. They wanted to find out the identity of the man financing the production of the drug and paying off the local law enforcement officers to look the other way.

Nick knew it was somebody local and he knew it had to be somebody who had power and influence in the small town, but damned if he could figure out who it was. Eventually he'd know, unless his cover was blown and he wound up dead.

"Container 57322 cleared." Lynn's voice pulled him from his inner thoughts.

He checked his watch. Twenty minutes left and four containers to go. She needed to be out of there by three o'clock because of the shift change that would take place at three-thirty.

And he needed to be out of here so he could get back to Raymore well before dawn. He didn't want one of his fellow thugs to drive by his house, see his car gone and wonder where in the hell he was.

"Nick? I hope you aren't going through my underwear drawer or drinking all my beer while you're cooling your heels in my luxury apartment."

He smiled, knowing she was attempting to alleviate the tension of the situation. The only way his tension would be eased was when she walked back through the door.

"Come on, get those last containers checked and get the hell out of there," he said.

He got up from the table, unable to sit as the next few minutes ticked by. "Come on, come on," he muttered as he paced in front of the window, checking his watch every few seconds.

"Container 57323 clear."

He heard the faint sound of the door closing on the container.

"Oh shit." The two words were uttered in a whisper filled with dread.

Nick froze and stared at the speaker. His heart nearly stopped as he heard the low, unmistakable sound of a dog growling.

Chapter 7

The dog stood about four feet away from her, barely visible in the night except for the pair of glowing gold eyes and gleaming sharp teeth that gnashed the air.

As a batch of clouds moved away from the moon, a faint illumination reached the ground and let her see that the dog was a Doberman. A *big* Doberman. He stood waist-high, ears alert and sharp teeth bared.

Terror ricocheted through her and all the blood seemed to leave her head, making her both nauseous and light-headed. She closed her eyes, fighting against the overwhelming, near-incapacitating fear.

Show him who is boss, stare him down.

No, don't meet his gaze. Staring at him will be a direct challenge.

Stare at him.

Look at the ground.

Lynn remained frozen stiff as she tried to remember everything she'd ever heard about encountering a mean dog. He growled again, a low, throaty sound of menace.

Hadn't she read somewhere that dogs could smell fear? God, could he smell the fear that climbed up her throat, twisted in her stomach? The stench of terror had to be rolling off her.

At least he hadn't barked. Barking would bring more trouble in the form of guards with guns. At the moment the dog seemed satisfied just growling and keeping her from moving.

But, she couldn't stay here forever. Seconds were ticking by. It was time for her to get the hell out of the yard.

The dog had her backed up against one of the containers so she couldn't back away from him. Nor could she go through him. She was fast, but she wasn't sure she could outrun gnashing teeth.

Sweat once again trickled down the center of her back, along the hairline of her brow. She'd never forgotten the sting of that childhood bite from the poodle, with sharp little teeth. She couldn't imagine what the Doberman's huge teeth would feel like biting into her tender skin.

Dawnie should be here. Although Lynn would

never wish her sister in harm's way, dogs didn't like Dawn. She frightened them. The sisters had all speculated that dogs sensed Dawn's genetic healing power and didn't know what to make of her. As a result they cowered away from her as if unsure of her species.

Unfortunately, dogs didn't have the same reaction to Lynn. Rather than cowering, the Doberman looked wickedly eager with the anticipation of enjoying her as his next savory meal.

She slowly drew in a breath through her nose, trying to steady her nerves, trying to figure out exactly how to get out of this particular predicament.

The only way out was up. Slowly, almost imperceptibly, she tilted her head back to look up at the roof of the container directly behind where she stood.

The growling grew louder and the dog took one step toward her. She could smell the fetid heat of his breath as he tensed his haunches and she knew their impasse was about to come to an end.

Not giving herself time to think she whirled around and jumped, gasping in relief as her fingers grasped the top of the container. As her fingers made the connection, she drew her legs up beneath her, not wanting anything to dangle low enough that it could be eaten.

The dog hit the side of the container with enough force to create a tin echo. The minute she was up on the roof, the dog began to bark. Sharp, piercing barks split the silence of the night. Lynn knew she had only seconds before somebody came to check out what was causing the dog's agitation.

She moved fast, jumping from the roof of one container to another and another. Her breaths came in sharp gasps that caused a pain in her side, but she kept moving.

When she reached the container closest to the corner where she had entered the yard she realized the dog had been left behind, confused as to her where-abouts.

Afraid of catching a bullet in the back, frantic with the need to get out, she leaped to the top of the concrete enclosure and fell to the other side.

She picked herself up and ran like the wind for three long blocks and only then did she slow to catch her breath. "I'm out," she managed to gasp and slammed her back against an abandoned building as her legs threatened to buckle.

Leaning forward at the waist, she drew in deep breaths of air, focusing on breathing through her nose instead of gasping from her mouth.

At least she'd managed to get most of the contain-ers cleared before the dog had found her. God, that had been too close. The flash of those awful snarling teeth still filled her head.

How was she going to get through the next week or two without once again encountering one of the guard dogs? She shoved off from the building and headed home.

The bar at the corner across from her apartment

building was closed and she encountered nobody on the streets. She checked her watch and saw that it was ten minutes until three. If it hadn't been for the dog she would have managed to clear all the containers she was supposed to for the night.

As it was she'd have two to add to her list for tomorrow night.

The only lights on in the apartment building were a dim one in the lobby and the one that shone from her window where Nick would be waiting for her.

As she rode up in the elevator to the third floor she tried to calm down, but the adrenaline that had spiked through her at the sight of that dog still rode through her veins like liquid energy.

When she reached her apartment door she raised her hand to knock, but the door flew open before her hand could connect with the wood.

"Are you okay?" Nick asked as she swept past him.

"I'm fine." She dropped the scanner on the table, then added the phone and the tiny transmitter, as well.

"That was tense." He raked a hand across his jaw, stress deepening the lines in his face.

"If you think it was tense from here, you should have been there. Jesus, I feel like I just outran the hounds of hell." She plopped down on the sofa and tried to still the trembling that threatened to take control of her limbs.

He sat next to her, some of the stress leaving his features. "What happened?"

She quickly told him about the dog and how she had managed to get away by taking the high road over the tops of the containers.

"You did a good job tonight."

She frowned. "I left two containers unchecked. Damn that dog."

"You managed to get through eleven without being caught. I'd say we can count this night as a success."

She got up from the sofa, wound too tight to sit still for any length of time. It had been a long time since she'd felt like this. She felt high, pumped with energy she didn't know how to diffuse.

"Are you sure you're all right?" Nick checked his watch and also got up from the sofa.

"I'm fine. I'm just pumped and trying to figure out if maybe I got sloppy, got noisy and that's what made the dog find me. Some of those doors on the containers squeak and creak as they're opened." She frowned thoughtfully. "I'll just need to be more careful tomorrow night."

"I wish I was the one out there searching the containers." His gaze was dark, brooding. "I wish anyone else was doing this but you. I don't like the danger this puts you in."

"It beats the alternative, which would probably be twenty-five years in prison," she replied.

Torment filled his eyes. "I wish things were different, I wish they'd left you alone."

There was no denying the caring that she saw in his gaze, the protective tenderness she felt emanating from him. "There have been a lot of times in the past year when I wished things were different."

She took a step closer to him, the surge of adrenaline transforming into something quite different. Desire. It struck her hard and fast in the very center of her being. She wanted to be in his arms. She wanted his mouth hot against hers, his body taking full possession of hers.

He must have read her desire, for his eyes blazed darker than ever and she recognized her want mirrored in him. "Do you still own your beach cottage?" She took another step closer. The air between them sizzled, taut with tension.

"Yeah." The single word whispered out of him as his chest rose and fell more rapidly than it had only moments before.

"I wish we were there now…just the two of us like it was before."

A muscle ticked in his jaw and she knew he was remembering the time they'd spent there making love.

To her disappointment he took a step back from her.

"Lynn, I don't want you to get hurt again."

She frowned. "Are you…are you in love with somebody else?" Just because she hadn't been with anyone since him didn't mean he hadn't found a new love.

"No." He took another step backward, as if not trusting himself to be too close to her. His gaze held hers intently. "I've only been in love once in my life, but we can't do this. Not now, not while we're in the middle of an assignment." He checked his watch again. "Besides, I've got to get out of here now."

"Where do you go when you leave here? To your cottage? Are you living there full-time?" She realized she had no idea what his life was like now. When he'd worked for Jonas he'd split his time between his cottage and a high-rent apartment near Jonas's house.

"No, I'm living someplace else." He frowned. "Don't ask me questions, Lynn, because I can't answer them right now. If I tell you anything at all about what I'm doing, where I go from here, then I put other people at risk."

It was easy for her to surmise that he must be working another job and in that instant she was afraid for him. "Am I putting you in danger?"

A knot appeared in his jaw. "I can handle it."

"Nick, I could work with somebody else if this is going to bring trouble to you."

His eyes flashed. "I said I can handle it. We'll see this through together." He walked over to the door and opened it. "I'll see you tomorrow night."

She locked up after him, then went to the window and stared out. Three stories below she watched him leave the building and get into an old clunker parked across the street.

When his car had pulled away from the curb and disappeared around the corner, she moved away from the window and sank down on the sofa. It was as if, when he'd left, he'd sucked the adrenaline right from her body and all she felt now was sheer exhaustion.

He'd confused her. His warm gaze had spoken of desire, but his actions had said something quite different. She roused herself from the sofa and removed the cushions to pull it out into a bed.

Sleep. That's what she needed now. She'd think about Nick in the morning.

She dreamed of gnashing teeth and exploding bombs and Nick. She woke up at noon, stiff from the too-thin mattress and hard springs and haunted by her dreams of death and destruction and a sense of unfinished business where Nick was concerned.

As she waited for the coffee to brew she wondered what kind of operation Nick was currently working. When she'd requested him as her partner she hadn't considered what else might be happening in his life.

The last thing she'd want to do was put him in a position that compromised his safety. She'd rather work alone than put him in danger.

It felt rather decadent, to be in her red silk nightgown at noon. She'd always been an early riser and it felt odd to look at the clock and see afternoon arriving with her first cup of coffee.

She was still seated at the table enjoying a second cup of coffee when she heard a knock. She froze, wondering who it could be. Before she could rise, a second knock resounded.

"Just a minute," she yelled. Maybe it was Nick telling her there had been a change of plans, or Blake, calling off the whole operation. Even as she thought of these scenarios she knew they weren't probable.

Making sure the chain was secured, she unlocked the dead bolt and eased the door open to see a huge man with a headful of unruly black hair and a tattoo of a teardrop at the outside corner of one of his eyes.

"The name is Tiny," he said. "I live in the apartment next door and I came to welcome you to the neighborhood." His voice was deep and graveled, like a man who had smoked for many years.

He wasn't your average kind of welcome committee volunteer and Lynn certainly wasn't looking to make new friends, especially with men who looked as though they'd just as soon rip your head off as talk to you.

Still, she didn't want to be rude or piss off a man who lived next door, a man who looked as if he could make her life here miserable if he so chose.

"It's nice to meet you, Tiny." She offered him a tentative smile even though she kept a firm grasp on the door. "I'm Lynn."

His gaze slid down the length of her, then back up to meet hers. "You a working girl?"

"Well, currently I'm unemployed but...oh, oh no," Lynn protested as she suddenly realized what he meant. He must have caught a glimpse of her nightgown and thought she might be a hooker.

"I just wanted to introduce myself and leave this flyer for you." He passed a folded green sheet of paper through the crack in her door. "If you feel the need for a little ministering, come see me. The church is located just a block east from here."

"Thanks," Lynn said, relieved when he moved away from her door. She carried the flyer back to the table and opened it. It was advertising the Christian Ministry under the leadership of Reverend Tiny Taylor, with services every night at seven.

So, the big, tough-looking man was a minister. Interesting. A jailhouse convert? She'd heard that the teardrop tattoo next to the eye meant the person wearing the tattoo had killed somebody. So who had the good Reverend killed? An unrepentant acquaintance?

She shoved the flyer aside, finished her coffee then went into the bathroom for a quick shower. Half an hour later, clad in jeans and a sleeveless red blouse, she once again sat at the table and booted up her computer.

She'd work awhile on the Chastain Web site, then spend the rest of the afternoon on the Spider files. She loved building Web sites, using her creativity to give birth to something colorful and stimulating. But, no matter how hard she tried to concentrate on Web building, thoughts of Nick kept intruding.

That there was still a huge amount of desire

between them was evident. But, that didn't mean she should allow her heart to get involved with him again. If she'd learned anything in the past year and a half it was that blind trust was a bad thing.

Even though she had once trusted Nick with her life, her heart and her soul, that didn't mean things could ever be the same again between them. She still sensed secrets in him, secrets beyond whatever assignment he was working on separate from her.

A year could bring a lot of changes in a man and she had no idea what influences, what circumstances Nick had faced in the last year. Even though she wanted to trust him wholly, blindly, she didn't.

She couldn't.

But, that didn't mean she didn't want to sleep with him again. Even now, just thinking about being in his arms and tasting the heat of his mouth, she was filled with a desire that she hadn't felt since the last time she'd seen him.

She wanted him and she was determined to have him at least one more time before all was said and done. He'd been a piece of unfinished business in her past and one way or another this time she intended to finish it.

She reached a good stopping point with the Web building and turned her attention to the Spider files. She had a dozen programs for decoding and decrypting files loaded onto her laptop. Yesterday she had only managed to run one of them. Today she hoped to get through a couple more and hopefully discover the key to whatever code had been used.

It was tedious work, but kept her mind off both Nick and the task she'd have to undertake in the wee hours of the morning.

By six o'clock, having no success with the files, she turned off her computer and fixed herself a large salad for dinner.

After eating, she paced the floor of the studio apartment with restless energy. It was still hours before Nick would arrive and the night would unfold and she was bored and felt the need to get out of the confines of the small apartment.

She wasn't used to so much alone time. At home her phone rang often and Leo drifted in and out to break the monotony.

Her gaze fell on the green flyer and she walked over and picked it up. Maybe she could waste a little time at the Christian Ministry listening to Reverend Tiny. It sure beat watching the roaches party in this dreary place. It also beat sitting around here ruminating about Nick.

Decision made, she changed out of her jeans and into a long black skirt, even though she assumed that at a church in an area like this the dress code was quite lax.

At quarter to seven she left the apartment, grateful to be outside despite the fact that the night air was filled with unpleasant scents and the faraway sounds of a car alarm beeping. In the distance a dog barked, adding to the sound of the music that drifted from the open door of the nearby bar.

A cool breeze came off the water and she welcomed the feel on her bare arms. One of Lynn's genetic gifts—or curses, as it were—was that even her sense of touch was more sensitive than normal. She felt physical contact more intensely than other people did.

Like her acute sense of hearing, she had learned to shut off her intense sensory perception in order to survive daily life.

Thankfully the church was in the opposite direction of the tavern where despite the early-evening hour things were beginning to hop.

The address on the flyer turned out to be a small storefront on which the words Christian Ministry had been spray-painted in bold black block letters across a picture window.

She opened the door and stepped inside. The room contained folding chairs set up theater style and a raised pulpit at the front of the room.

Three people were seated on the chairs, an old man who smiled wearily at her, a young man who appeared to be between the ages of thirteen and fifteen and a young woman who sported a swollen split lip.

She slid into a chair at the back of the room just as Reverend Tiny walked in from a doorway near the pulpit. Again she was struck by the bulk of the man. He looked better suited to a wrestling ring than a church.

His nose looked as if it had been broken more

than once and his bulging biceps and tree-trunk size thighs probably kept anyone from screwing with him. Tonight he was clad in a lightweight tan suit and a white shirt and looked almost presentable.

"I see we're a small group tonight," he said after nodding to each of the attendees. "But, Jesus never cared how big or small the crowd he spoke with was and neither do I."

It had been a long time since Lynn had listened to a sermon. Jonas had never been a churchgoer and so Lynn's spiritual education had been sadly lacking when she'd been growing up.

It wasn't until she was in college that she'd started attending church on a regular basis and had found the church community a welcoming place.

She listened to Tiny as he spoke of forgiveness and salvation. It had taken her the better part of a year to find forgiveness in her heart for Jonas and the men and women from Lab 33 who had played God with her life.

But with the help of her sisters and the Cassandras, she'd realized that holding on to the kind of anger she'd felt was counterproductive and would only eventually destroy her.

When Tiny was finished with his sermon, he indicated that cookies and coffee would be served for those who wanted to stick around.

Reluctant to hurry back to her apartment, Lynn stayed and helped herself to a cookie and a cup of coffee from the table to the right of the pulpit.

"I see you decided to join us tonight." Tiny smiled at her as he picked up a cookie. He turned to the only one who had remained behind besides Lynn, the old man. "This is Joseph. Joseph, Lynn. She's new to the neighborhood."

Joseph smiled at Lynn. "You look like a nice girl. My advice to you would be to get out of this neighborhood as soon as you can."

"That's my plan," Lynn said. She couldn't wait to get back to her life in Phoenix. "Is the crowd always this small?"

"It varies," Tiny said. "We usually have our biggest crowd on Monday nights, when people are looking to atone for their weekend sins."

"Wednesday nights are always slow," Joseph said. "Folks have already forgotten about last weekend's sins and they haven't committed next weekend's sins yet." He looked at Tiny. "I'll go ahead and start putting away the cookies."

"How long have you been doing this?" Lynn asked Tiny as Joseph began to pack the cookies away in a plastic container.

"Two years. I grew up in this neighborhood. Worked the docks, drank too much, drugged too much and wound up killing a man in that tavern on the corner."

He grimaced, as if the memory pained him. "He was a local thug and so was I. He mouthed off, threw a punch and I broke a bottle over his head. Killed him. I spent ten years in prison and had lots of time to decide where I wanted to go with my life when I got out. Decided to come back here and try to make a difference."

"Are you?"

He shrugged his massive shoulders. "Did you see that boy who was here? His name is Jessie. His father is a drunk and his mama is a crack whore. Statistics say he's a lost soul, that he'll probably wind up in a gang, in prison or dead before he's eighteen. But, every night, instead of running the streets, he comes here. He eats dinner with me, listens to me lecture him, then he goes home and studies. I like to think I'm making a difference." He crooked a dark eyebrow. "What about you? Are you a lost soul?"

"No, just temporarily displaced." Lynn offered him a tentative smile. "Well, thanks for the sermon and the cookie."

"You're welcome here any night of the week. You have any problems, you come see me. I take care of my flock."

Chapter 8

"I brought you more presents," Nick said when he arrived at the apartment at eleven-thirty the next evening. He looked fine in a pair of worn jeans and a black T-shirt that exposed muscled biceps and forearms. He carried with him a plastic bag. He set the bag on the table then gestured for her to join him at the table.

"Oh goody, you know how much I love presents. So, what did you bring?" She sat and looked at him expectantly.

"First of all I have the latest photo of the containers that were unloaded today." He pulled the photo out of the plastic grocery bag.

She studied the photo for a minute, noting the location of the newest containers. "How do you get these?" she asked curiously.

"They're in my car each night when I get in to drive here. I have no idea who delivers them, they're just there. And now, I have another surprise for you." He reached into the plastic bag and removed a smaller bag containing two thick slabs of meat. "A couple of nice Kansas City strip steaks."

"You brought me steaks?" She raised an eyebrow. "Does this mean you're planning on cooking for me?"

He smiled, that lazy upturn of the corners of his lips that always shot a tiny thrill through her. "I can either cook them for you while you're gone or you can take them with you and give them to the hounds from hell."

"Ah, you sure know the way to a girl's heart."

"Speaking of hearts, who's Leo?"

The swift change of subject caused her to sit back in her chair and blink in surprise. "Leo? He lives in the apartment next door to me, in Phoenix. Why? How do you know him?"

"I don't. But when I showed up at your apartment door the other day you said something about not sleeping with him." Although his expression remained placid, that telltale muscle tightened in his jaw.

She thought about teasing him, giving him the impression that she'd been sleeping with Leo, but she wasn't the kind of woman to play those kinds of games. "Leo's a very nice man who has indicated he'd like to have a relationship with me."

"And would you like that?" The jaw muscle ticked faster.

"If I wanted that, then I wouldn't have been yelling through the door that I wasn't going to sleep with him," she said. "Leo is good-looking and wonderfully uncomplicated, but he doesn't make my heart beat faster and he doesn't make my breath catch in my chest."

She got up from the table and walked to the window, where she peered out into the darkness of the night. She could die tonight. She'd be a fool not to recognize the possibility of her own demise, especially under the circumstances.

She turned back to face Nick. In the brief time they'd spent together she'd felt the awkwardness of a past unfinished and it was suddenly important to her that she tell him how she felt about seeing him again.

"Nick, I want you to know something." She returned to the table and sat across from him. "There have been many nights in the past year that I've been filled with regret, that I wished somehow that I hadn't left Miami, that I hadn't left you."

His features twisted into a semblance of pain. "Lynn, we can't change the past. You needed to go. If you remember, I encouraged you to go. I knew you needed to find out things that I couldn't find out for you." His warm gaze caressed her features. "It wouldn't have worked if you'd stayed. Your questions would have eaten you alive and you would have come to resent me."

She sighed. "You're probably right." She looked at her watch then touched the back of his hand. His skin burned warm beneath her fingertips. His gaze darkened at her touch and sparked with something she recognized as desire.

He pulled his hand away from hers. "It's time for you to go."

"I know." Reluctantly she stood once again and picked up the bag of steaks. Always when the conversation got too personal, he jumped into business mode. "Hopefully I'll see you back here around three."

"Be careful."

"Always." She walked to the door and opened it, then turned back to look at him. "There's just one more thing I want you to know in case anything happens to me. I never stopped wanting you, Nick." She didn't wait for him to answer, but instead turned and left the apartment.

Minutes later she hit the street and broke into a run, wondering what affect, if any, her words had had on him. She'd thought she'd known him better than anyone on the face of the earth a year ago. But she couldn't get a handle on the man he was now.

He'd told her he was working another assignment and she respected that he couldn't talk to her about that. Just as she couldn't mention working on the Spider files to him. But, she had the crazy feeling that his secrecy went beyond whatever assignment he was working.

He wasn't giving up anything of himself, except

during those moments when she was certain she felt desire for her wafting from him.

With conscious effort she dismissed thoughts of Nick from her mind, knowing it would be a mistake to work the yard while distracted.

She went over the wall of the holding area in the same place she had the night before. She hit the ground and froze, listening to her surroundings.

Thankfully there was no pitter-patter of any four-legged creatures, nor was there any sound to indicate any human presence.

She got to work.

Ten containers had been unloaded that day and she had the two containers remaining from the night before. She went to those two first.

By the time she was on her third container of the night she felt herself falling into a rhythm. Get in, run the scanner and get out. Get in, run the scanner and get out. And after clearing each one, she whispered the number of the container aloud so that Nick could check her progress and keep track of the cleared items.

As she moved from spot to spot in the enclosure, she sometimes heard the voices of guards nearby, but they never got close enough to even make her heart beat faster.

By two o'clock she'd finished her night's work without encountering either the guards or drawing the attention of the dogs. She left the yard and headed back toward her apartment.

"Mission accomplished," she said into her transmitter. "I'm on my way back."

She'd moved unusually fast while conducting her search and so she walked down the quiet, dark sidewalk at a slower pace in order to catch her breath.

As she walked past the buildings she heard a variety of sounds. Air conditioners hummed, cooling the air inside the dreary places. The sound of a woman laughing drifted from an opened window. A dog barked someplace in the distance. Normal sounds that helped dispel the adrenaline that had hyped her up while she'd worked.

A baby cried from one of the buildings that looked abandoned and she heard the shushing tones of an older woman. Hell of a place to raise a baby, she thought.

The night was warm and more humid than usual. The air wrapped around her with a closeness that made her feel slightly claustrophobic. The weatherman had forecast storms later in the week. During her years of living in Miami, she'd survived too many hurricanes not to take storms quite seriously.

Her apartment building came into sight and she saw the light in her window spilling out into the night. She'd managed to get through the night unscathed and that light represented safety and Nick.

Nick. Damn the man anyway. Every time she looked at him she remembered how good he'd been as a lover and she wanted him again. If nothing else came from their time working together, she was determined to make love to him once more, to see if her memories were as good as reality or had simply been magnified in the time that had gone by.

"New girl on the block needs to understand who owns these streets."

The venomous voice came from behind Lynn, startling her. She whirled around and caught a glimpse of the hooker she'd seen the first night she'd arrived before a fist slammed into her face.

Pain exploded under her right eye and she reeled backward with the force of the blow. She would have fallen if not for a trash can she crashed into with a bang.

She grabbed the can and steadied herself as the woman came at her again with fists raised to strike. Tonight the hooker was dressed in a short red sequined dress, but it was obvious she didn't have loving on her mind.

"What is your problem?" Lynn exclaimed to the woman whose features were twisted in a mask of cold rage. Jesus, she could feel a trickle of blood running down her cheek. She swiped at it with the back of one hand.

"You're my problem. You're out here prancing your ass in those tight little pants and you gotta know these streets are mine and Stella don't share." She swung wildly at Lynn, who easily sidestepped the blow.

"Look, lady, don't make me hurt you," Lynn warned. As mean and crazy as Stella appeared with her dark eyes narrowed and her mouth twisted into a grimace of malevolence, Lynn knew with a well-placed kick she could seriously harm the woman.

"A little-ass girl like you think you're going to hurt me?" Stella laughed. "I'm going to bust you up, bitch, just so you understand the way things are." With a roar of rage, Stella charged her, arms swinging and fists clenched.

Lynn didn't shy away, knowing that unless she intended to tangle with Stella every night while she was in this place she needed to take care of the situation now.

Unlike the Doberman whose gaze she'd avoided, she stared Stella in her wild eyes, aware that she was encouraging a confrontation rather than avoiding one. It was the only way to resolve the issue.

She managed to dodge a right cross, then grabbed one of Stella's wrists and held on tight. Stella tried to hit her with the other hand, but Lynn evaded the blows.

She squeezed Stella's wrist painfully tight and the woman yelped in pain, her knees buckling and hitting the sidewalk. "Listen to me," Lynn said through clenched teeth. "You don't know who you're messing with."

"Let me go. You're gonna break my wrist," Stella moaned and tried to twist away.

"I'm not letting you go until you understand that I'm not working the streets, I'm not cutting into your business. I'll leave you alone if you leave me alone. Got it?"

Stella nodded vigorously, her large breasts

heaving beneath the red sequined top. "Okay…okay. It's all good. Just stop hurting me."

Lynn let go of her wrist. Stella collapsed onto the pavement for a moment, then jumped up and faced her, a wicked-looking knife appearing in her hand. "You're dead, girlfriend."

A cold wave swept over Lynn as Stella rushed her. Praying her aim would be good, Lynn delivered a right-legged kick that connected with Stella's hand. The knife flew from her grasp and clattered to the street out of reach.

Stella gasped just before a roundhouse kick hit her on the side of the head. She fell to the pavement like a sack of rocks.

Lynn hurried to her side, relieved to see she was alive and still conscious, although obviously dazed. She leaned down and stared the woman in the eyes. "Like I said before, you leave me alone and I'll leave you alone, got it?"

Stella made a faint nod, all trace of anger gone from her features. As she sat up and rubbed the side of her head where Lynn had kicked her, Lynn took off down the sidewalk.

She stopped in the street and picked up the knife, then continued on her way. As she crossed the street to get to her apartment building she glanced back and saw no sign of Stella.

Nick greeted her at her apartment door. "You're bleeding." He took her by the arm and led her to the sofa, then went to the sink and wet a dish towel.

"I'm fine." She dropped the knife on the coffee table, then reached to touch her upper cheek. "She must have been wearing a ring when she hit me. And by the way, thanks for your help."

"Actually, I was just about to head out the door to help you when I heard you take her down," he replied.

He sat on the sofa next to her and wiped at the wound. She closed her eyes, allowing him to gently clean her cheek. "They warned me about dogs and guards and bombs, but nobody said anything about crazy, territorial hookers," she said dryly.

She opened her eyes to see him smile. "Ah, she was just jealous because you look better in tight pants." He dabbed at her cheek again. "I think you could use some ice on this." He got up and went to the refrigerator.

When he returned to the sofa he had an ice cube wrapped in a dish towel. He pressed it to her cheek, his gaze soft as it lingered on her. "How did she manage to sneak up on you?"

Lynn sighed in frustration. "I don't know. I guess I was distracted." She couldn't very well tell him that she'd been thinking about him, that she'd been contemplating making love with him again.

She frowned. "It was stupid of me. It was my fault for shutting down before I was back here safe and sound." Even now it was difficult to think of anything but Nick's nearness to her. "I completely tuned out. It was a stupid mistake."

He sat so close to her, his thigh pressed against

hers, and the heat of that contact made her heart race. As he pressed the icy cloth against her cheek, she covered his hand with hers.

"Talk to me, Nick," she said and sighed wearily. "We haven't really talked." She pulled his hand from her cheek.

"What do you want to talk about?" He got up and put the ice and cloth into the sink, then returned to the sofa next to her.

"I don't know. Talk to me about what your life has been like the last year. Tell me how your family is doing, if you still go to that seafood place on the beach. Just talk to me about anything other than pissed-off hookers and shipping containers and mad dogs."

He smiled, a gentle smile of understanding. "For the last year I've pretty much done nothing but work. For the first couple of months after you left Miami I spent most of my time trying to hunt down Jonas. The CIA took over when he surfaced in Berzhaan."

Despite the fact that Lynn had participated in a sting operation that involved her luring her godfather to Nick's cottage where a dozen FBI agents awaited to arrest him, he'd managed to evade capture. Actually, he'd used Lynn as a hostage to get away. Eventually he'd been killed overseas in the Middle Eastern country of Berzhaan, where he'd been dealing arms with insurgents. Lynn had thought it poetic justice when an Athena Academy grad, FBI legal Selera Shaw Jones, had played a big part in foiling the attempted coup that led to Jonas's death.

"As for my family, you know that my father passed away. My mother is doing well. She moved to a retirement village in New Mexico and I think that for the first time in many years she's enjoying life. My sister got married and seems happy, as well. Without my father's influence, my brother, Tony, is trying to walk the straight and narrow." His eyes flashed darkly.

"What? Tell me?"

"That's what they used as a threat to get me to talk to you."

"Your brother?" Lynn frowned, wanting to understand.

He nodded. "You know my old man walked outside the law, and while he was alive Tony walked there with him. Tony was too weak to buck the powerful Joey Barnes. He's getting his life together now, working a legitimate job, but they told me they had enough information on him to put him in prison if I didn't cooperate with them."

"They have no heart," she said, indignant on his behalf.

Nick shrugged. "They do what they need to do to get a job done. And as far as that seafood place, I haven't been back to Smokey's since the night I took you there and we danced together."

Memories flooded through her mind. His strong arms around her as he guided her across the dance floor with ease and grace. She'd fallen more than a little bit in love with him that night.

"What about your family?" he asked. "It must be great for you to have sisters."

Lynn smiled, the gesture turning into a wince as her cheek ached. "It's wonderful. They're amazing women, Nick. Faith works with the police department in New Orleans and is dating a detective there. Since the hurricane they're mostly involved in the cleanup work and getting the city back on its feet. Dawn does a lot of traveling, and she thinks maybe she recently got married to Captain Des Asher."

Nick raised a dark brow. "She thinks *maybe* she got married? She doesn't know for sure?"

"Des works for the British Special Air Services. The wedding ceremony was an elaborate scheme to smoke out an assassin. But, Dawn thinks Des hired a real minister instead of a fake one, and they had a marriage license as part of their cover. Which might make their marriage real instead of pretend."

"Is she upset about it?"

Lynn couldn't help the smile that once again took possession of her lips. "She says she is, but I think she secretly admires Des and his deviousness. From what she's told me about him, they make a good pair." Her smile fell away. "Personally, I wouldn't be so forgiving. After spending most of my life with Jonas, I don't tolerate liars in my life anymore."

She sat up straighter. "Did I tell you I met my father? I can't remember if I e-mailed you about him or not."

He shook his head. "You didn't."

"His name is Tom King. He's a Navy SEAL commander and he was the donor whose sperm Lab 33 stole and used to fertilize my mother's eggs. But more important he's a nice man. He's married to a wonderful woman named Ellen and they have a fifteen-year-old son."

"It must have been strange to meet him after all this time," he said.

"It was, but strange in a nice kind of way." She couldn't help but smile as she thought of Tom. "We're still working on building a relationship. He didn't even know the three of us existed. But we have his eyes. He has the same green-gold eyes as me and my sisters."

Her gaze fell on the clock on the end table. Ten after three. "And now you've got to get out of here." How she wished he could stay. How she wished they could talk all night.

"Yeah, I do." There was a touch of reluctance in his voice. He stood. She walked with him to the door and once there he touched her cheek lightly. "You'd better get some more ice on that. It's swelling a bit."

She reached up and captured his hand once again with her own. "Don't look so worried. I'm going to survive this just fine. I'm a lot tougher than anything these streets or this assignment can throw my way."

"I hope you're right. God, I hope you're right."

Neither of them moved and she thought he might kiss her. He leaned closer to her, his dark eyes radiating with intent.

She held her breath, wanting him to crush his

mouth to hers, needing him to momentarily take her away from this place and this time with the magic of his kiss.

But, instead of kissing her, he pulled his hand from hers and stepped out the door. "Until tomorrow," he said, then disappeared down the dim hallway.

Lynn closed her door and slammed home the dead bolt. Damn the man anyway. With the single touch of his hand against her face, he lit a fire in her. He was the only man she'd ever met who made her think of rumpled sheets and mind-shattering climaxes.

She stalked over to the refrigerator and pulled out a tray of ice cubes. She didn't know if she should apply one to her injured cheek or dump a dozen ice cube trays in the bottom of the shower and swim in it in an effort to douse the flames he stirred in her.

A year ago Nick had been ordered by his superiors to seduce her in an effort to give him an in into Jonas's operation of illegal activities.

Lynn stuck an ice cube against her cheek and frowned thoughtfully. Maybe it was time for a bit of "turnabout is fair play." Maybe a little seduction was in order on her part, not because anyone had ordered it, but because she wanted it.

One thing Lynn had learned from the Athena women was that if you wanted something you'd better go after it; nobody was going to hand you anything on a silver platter. Not anything that truly mattered, anyway.

She walked over to the window and stared down

on the empty streets. The ice melted quickly, releasing cold water that ran down her cheek.

When the cube was no bigger than her thumb, she tossed it into the sink and returned to the window. These were mean streets, not fit for people. She touched her cheek and winced.

She wasn't mad at Stella. The woman was protecting what little she had against a perceived threat. In truth, Lynn felt sorry for the woman.

Eventually Lynn would leave here, but people like Stella would remain, fighting for what little life gave to them. With a sigh, she turned and went into the small bathroom to change into her nightclothes.

"Wow," Lynn muttered aloud as she stared at the list of names that appeared on the computer screen in front of her. She'd been working the Spider files since dawn, running first one program, then another in an effort to break whatever code had been used. An adjustment to one of her programs had finally been rewarded with a breakthrough.

A burst of euphoria electrified her. Although the adjusted program hadn't decoded much, it had given up a new list of names. And quite a list it was, too.

She leaned back in her chair and frowned thoughtfully as she gazed at the names she'd uncovered. Jeffrey Carson. Malcom Gerrer. Scott Hafford. Thomas Ridgewater.

She recognized all of the names. Carson was a Federal Judge. Gerrer was a senator from the state of

Missouri. She thought Hafford was some kind of military contractor and Ridgewater was a well-known, high-profile attorney who was often in the news.

Why would these people's names be in a file that had come from Lab 33? Had they helped to fund the unholy lab? Running a finger across her lower lip she frowned thoughtfully. What did it mean? Unfortunately the list was all that particular program had managed to decode.

She had just finished e-mailing the list to Delphi when someone rapped on her door. She looked at the clock in the lower right corner of her computer screen. Just after ten. Now what?

Before answering she closed the program she'd been running and pulled up her screen saver of dancing dolphins.

She cracked open the door to see Tiny. He seemed to fill all the spaces in the door frame. "Heard you had a little trouble last night." He held up a packaged cinnamon coffee cake. "I brought you a little sweet to take away the sting of the fight with Stella."

Lynn unchained the door and opened it to allow him inside, as always slightly put off by his huge size. "I'm a sucker for coffee cake." She gestured to the table. "Sit down and I'll make some coffee."

In truth she welcomed the break from work, from her thoughts, and from the isolation she felt cooped up inside the apartment. Despite the fact that she was excited about her success, she was ready for a break.

"How did you hear about my little tangle with Stella?" she asked.

"I make it my business to know what happens on these streets. Looks like Stella got in a good shot."

Lynn raised a hand to her cheek and smiled ruefully. "Only one. She sucker punched me. I never even saw it coming."

Tiny shook his head and opened the coffee cake container as Lynn got out a couple of plates and forks from the cabinet. "When she told me what she had done, I told her she was way out of line. Fists and such are never the way to solve an issue. Believe me, I know." He frowned darkly as if remembering a particularly bleak time in his life.

"She obviously felt threatened by my presence here. She was protecting her territory." Lynn turned to the counter and began to prepare the coffee. "I hope she gets it that I'm not looking to take over her business."

"So, what *are* you looking to do?"

She turned around to face him. "What do you mean?"

He shrugged his massive shoulders and his gaze held open speculation. "Just wondering what you're doing down here in this kind of neighborhood. That blouse you got on, I recognize the designer label. It cost more than a month's rent in this dive. And this computer—" he stabbed a thumb in the direction of the laptop "—quite a pricey item for a girl down on her luck."

Her mind raced and her heart did the same. This

was exactly what Blake had warned her about,
getting close to a neighbor, inviting confidences that
could be dangerous. It would be suspicious if she
didn't come up with an answer. A mix of truth and
fiction was in order, she quickly decided.

She turned back to the cabinet and withdrew two
coffee mugs and set them on the table. "My father
died several months ago. He was a very wealthy
man."

She pulled the carafe from the coffeemaker and
poured them each a cup of the fresh brew. "Cream
or sugar?"

"Nah, this is good." He cupped his massive hands
around the mug.

She joined him at the table, aware that he was
waiting for some sort of story that would explain her
presence here. "I had a great life while Dad was
alive. I had the best of everything that money could
buy. But, when he passed away I discovered all his
money had been gotten illegally and the authorities
moved in and took everything. All I managed to
keep were some clothes and personal items."

It was easy to interject bitterness into her voice.
She wasn't bitter about losing everything when
Jonas had gone down, but there was still a trace of
bitterness inside her over the fact that she didn't
believe he'd ever really loved her, he'd only loved
the skills she possessed to help him build his fortune.

"Tough break," Tiny said. "I think sometimes it's
harder to have the world by the ass and lose it than

to never have it at all." He cut them each a generous piece of the coffee cake.

"Thanks. Anyway, since Dad's death, I've been just knocking around, trying to figure out what I'm going to do. I never had a job and don't have any real skills except a bit of computer knowledge. I had just enough money left to rent this place for a couple of months." She pointed to the computer. "I'm hoping by that time I can get some business building Web sites for people."

"You know how to do all that computer stuff?" One of his thick dark brows rose upward.

She nodded. "I was taking computer classes when my father died. Unfortunately I had to drop out because I didn't have the money to continue, but I'm teaching myself everything I need to know. I'll never have what I had before, but I'm hoping I'll have better than this…no offense."

"None taken," he replied easily. "That's good, that you have a plan. The faster you get on your feet and out of here the better it will be for you. Stella, she's got no way out. She's third-generation hooker. It's the only kind of life she knows."

"Just let her know I'm not competition."

Tiny smiled, the gesture mitigating his badass aura. "That's the problem. Stella knows, if you work the streets, there *is* no competition. You're younger and new to the streets. She'd be out of work."

He leaned back in the chair, a thoughtful frown stretching across his broad forehead. "Stella, she does all right. She has her regulars, mostly dock-workers and for the most part they treat her real good. These streets are the only home she's known."

"She has nothing to worry about where I'm concerned," Lynn replied.

"So, what were you doing on the streets at three in the morning?" Although Tiny's tone was light and easy there was more than a hint of suspicion in his eyes.

She frantically searched her brain for a reasonable explanation. "I'm an insomniac," she replied. "I have trouble sleeping at night and the one thing that helps is if I run."

"Running around here at that time of the morning isn't exactly smart," he observed, then raised his mug to his mouth and took a sip.

"I'm pretty good when it comes to self-defense."

He lowered his mug and grinned. "That's what Stella said. She's as street tough as they come and she said you put her on her ass in five seconds flat."

"Because of my father's wealth, he believed I should be trained in all forms of self-defense." This much was true. Jonas had made sure that Lynn had the best training in all of the defense arts. "I can take care of myself."

He sipped his coffee, his gaze still on her over the rim of the mug. She had a feeling he didn't quite believe her stories.

"Your tattoo—didn't it hurt getting it there so close to your eye?" she asked, desperate to change the subject away from her.

He reached up and touched the teardrop tattoo. "Not really. At the time I got it done I was filled with such a rage that pain meant nothing to me." He dropped his hand but his eyes remained narrowed. "I was one badass dude before I went to prison and found God." He smiled. "But I'm a changed man now."

They were both silent for a few moments, each of them eating their coffee cake. She hoped he was a changed man. She hoped he'd bought the story she'd spun about what hard luck had brought her to the neighborhood. She also hoped he believed her insomnia tale.

She had a feeling that Tiny was a man who could either make her brief life here better or could seriously complicate everything for her.

Chapter 9

Nick stood against an inner wall inside the warehouse, watching the activity that took place around him. It was a workday for the drug dealers of Raymore and the air was rife with the acrid scent of chemicals.

Under normal circumstances Nick wouldn't be caught dead within a thousand yards of a meth lab. Practically every night of the week the news had at least one report of a meth lab blowing up.

The typical meth-maker either had no idea or didn't care about the dangers of the chemicals that were needed to make the drug. They had no idea how combustible those chemicals could be if not handled correctly.

The men working in the warehouse in Raymore weren't the normal, garden-variety dope dealers. The warehouse was outfitted with equipment to make it look more like a science laboratory than a den of iniquity.

Stainless steel sinks, glass beakers and shiny countertops had been installed to provide a clean environment and assure that the purest drug could be made without threat of contamination.

The chemicals were stored in separate rooms off the main lab, assuring no accidental mix that could prove deadly.

The operation took place about once a month, with both the powder and the coveted crystal form of the drug being made for distribution.

Like most of the men in the room, Nick was one of the mules. It was his job to move the product when it was ready. Even though he had nothing to do with the actual production, the man in charge insisted that all the men who worked for him be present on cooking day.

"Yo, Nicky."

Nick turned to see Jimmy Warren limping toward him. Jimmy grinned, looking far more boyish than his forty-three years. "Hey, Jimmy," Nick greeted him. "Leg bothering you tonight?"

Jimmy stood against the wall next to Nick and leaned over to rub down his right leg. "Damn thing always gives me more trouble than usual when there's rain in the forecast."

Jimmy was on social security disability due to an accident on the docks several years ago. His leg had been crushed, leaving him with a permanent limp. He supplemented his disability checks by being the number-two man in this operation.

"I was thinking maybe we'd get together a poker game tonight," Jimmy said as he straightened. "What do you say? Are you in?"

"I don't think so, Jimmy. I'm beat. I think when we're done here I'll just head home." The poker games rarely ended before midnight and Nick had another date to keep.

"Ah, come on, man. It will be fun. We'll drink some brews and play a little Texas Hold 'Em."

Nick shook his head. "Count me out. You know I've got no luck."

Jimmy laughed. "That ain't no shit. I've never seen anybody as unlucky as you and I'm not just talking about your poker playing."

Nick knew exactly what Jimmy was talking about. Nick had gone undercover on this job using his real name and his real background as the son of Joey Barnes, organized crime mobster.

Nick had let all these men know that he'd expected to take over his father's business when the old man had died, but his younger brother had frozen him out.

These men also knew that Nick had worked as a security expert for the powerful, wealthy Jonas White. Nick had told them that it had been a stroke of luck that the FBI hadn't been able to tie him to Jonas's illegal activities. It had been his misfortune that, just when Jonas was going to cut him in for big money, the man had disappeared.

That very background had given Nick enough credibility to get him into the heart of this operation. Now, if he could just identify Jimmy's boss, his work here would be done. The Feds could move in and arrest enough people to fill a small prison.

"You sure you won't change your mind?" Jimmy asked. "I mean, what else you got to do on a Saturday night?"

"Nothing, but I don't feel like playing tonight. I'm really tired. By the time we get finished here I'll be ready for bed."

Jimmy clapped him on the back. "You're getting old, Nicky boy. I guess if I want to take somebody's money tonight, it will have to be a fool other than you." With a laugh, Jimmy nodded a goodbye and headed across the room.

Nick narrowed his eyes and watched him go. Of all the men in the room, Jimmy wielded the most power, but he wasn't the man the FBI wanted.

Although they would be pleased to lock his ass up, along with every other ass in this place, they wanted the big man, the money man…the brains of the operation.

Every time they worked here in the warehouse Nick had the gut feeling that the big man was here, that he was smart enough, involved enough not to let anything happen that he didn't see or hear with his own eyes. But, who?

The butcher, the baker, the candlestick maker. They were all here, but none of them seemed bright enough to be the brains behind the brawn. Whoever had orchestrated all this was not only bright, but ballsy.

It took big ones to set up a drug operation in the middle of a small town. It took guts to wheel and deal with the local authorities and get them to look the other way.

In all his years of working for the FBI, Nick had never seen a town as corrupt as Raymore. It was rotten from the inside out and when arrests were finally made, half the town would find itself behind bars.

In the next couple of days each of the mules would be given a quantity of the meth to distribute to contacts around the country. Nick's contact was a Cuban street gang leader in an area of Miami known as Little Cuba.

What the people in Raymore didn't know was that the street punk had been turned around by the FBI and the drugs he got from Nick never made it to the streets. The FBI paid for the shipment with marked money that was brought back to Jimmy.

A wave of weariness swept over him. He was sick of these people, sick of the life he was living here. He trusted nobody, knew that to place trust in the wrong person could mean his death.

It was a hell of a way to live. That's what Lynn had said and she had been right. When he'd first met her, he'd felt as if he was on the brink of losing his humanity.

He'd been so focused on bringing down Jonas White he'd lost just a little bit of his soul to the job. Lynn had given that back to him with her charming innocence, her delightful laughter and her passionate love.

When she'd left Miami to search for her roots he'd crashed into a kind of despair he'd never experienced before. He'd never known loneliness until she'd left him. And in the weeks and months following her departure he'd taken the most dangerous jobs the bureau had to offer, as if risking his life might give some meaning to it.

Now he found himself wanting out...out of the danger, out of the stress. And that wasn't all he wanted. He wanted *her*. Damn, but he wanted Lynn with an intensity that made it difficult for him to concentrate, difficult for him to stay sane whenever he was around her.

Each night when she came back to the apartment from searching the containers, she smelled wild. The scent of the night wind and the crashing waves of the ocean clung to her, but beneath the wildness he smelled her, that particular fragrance that was hers alone.

It twisted in his gut, made the blood crash at his temples. His want of her was something raw and elemental and it ripped at him every minute of the day and night.

And she wanted him, too. He felt it in her fingertips whenever they happened to touch him. He saw it burning in those amazing green-gold eyes of hers.

It had been five nights since she'd tangled with the hooker and in the past five nights the tension between him and Lynn had grown to nearly intolerable heights.

Even now, just thinking about her, Nick felt a thick, hot surge of blood coursing through his veins and his head filled with fantasies he consciously shoved away.

The worst part about his job was that he'd been warned over and over again not to interfere if she should get into trouble. Listening to the growl of that dog coming over the speaker on her kitchen table had been difficult, but hearing the low, menacing voice of that hooker had been torturous.

If he hadn't firmly believed she could handle herself against a streetwalker, he wouldn't have been able to stay in the apartment and not go to her aid.

He rubbed a hand wearily across his forehead. He didn't mind risking his life here on this job, but for three hours a night as he waited in the apartment for Lynn to return safe and sound he suffered the worst kind of fear he'd ever known.

He shoved thoughts of Lynn away as Kip Laroson ambled over to where he stood. "Heard you're not in for the poker game tonight. We were all hoping to relieve you of some money."

Nick forced a smile as he eyed the tall, slender

redhead. Kip looked like an older version of Tom Sawyer. He had open, friendly features all covered with freckles. He looked like the boy next door unless you looked deep in his eyes. Kip had the coldest blue eyes Nick had ever seen.

"You took enough of my money the last time we played," he replied.

Kip laughed. "Yeah, as I recall we relieved you of a bundle the last time. But, it's not like you aren't making a good living. We all are, thanks to this." Kip turned his gaze to the activity going on in the room. "Although we can't be making half of what the main man is making. I'd like to know who's behind all this."

"Me, too," Nick replied. "Got any ideas?"

Kip turned to look at him again. "For a while I thought it was Mayor Winslowe, but that man is too damned stupid to run the city let alone an operation like this. Whoever it is, he only talks to Jimmy and according to Jimmy he's just a voice on the phone." Kip shrugged. "I guess it doesn't matter who's in charge as long as we're all getting paid well for our work."

"That's the way I look at it." Nick tamped down an edge of frustration. His associates at the FBI had checked out everyone in town looking for large sums of money in bank accounts, new expensive homes or cars, anything that would point to the man in charge. They'd found nothing. They were no closer now to discovering Mr. Big than they had been three months ago when Nick first breezed into town.

The day was long and busy and it wasn't until

eleven-thirty that night that Nick's head once again filled with thoughts of Lynn.

As he backed out of the driveway of the place he'd been living for the past three months, he thought of the brief time they'd spent together at his beach cottage.

He'd been happy there with her, happy as he'd never been before. Certainly his childhood hadn't been happy. Growing up with Joey Barnes for a father had been miserable. As Jonas had groomed Lynn to be his personal thief, Joey had tried to groom his eldest son in the business of organized crime. But, the last thing Nick had wanted to do was become his old man.

So, he'd left the family and without telling anyone he'd become an FBI agent. On the side, he'd opened up a security business as a front, and his family thought he was doing nothing more than selling security equipment to frightened home owners.

When he'd told his father he had no interest in following in his footsteps, he'd been cursed to hell and disowned. Nick had managed to maintain a relationship with his mother, brother and sister, but it had been difficult.

Lynn had filled the emptiness in his life, an emptiness that had been with him since he'd been a young boy and realized his father wasn't any kind of a role model.

A bolt of lightning sizzled across the sky followed by a crash of thunder. He tightened his grip on the steering wheel, his gaze divided between the highway and the approaching storm.

The storm was supposed to have moved in a couple of days ago, but had stalled out in the ocean. The weathermen had indicated that it was on the move once again and due to hit sometime tonight.

He felt as if the storm was inside him, building and building until it would explode. But he couldn't allow that to happen. He had to remain in control.

There was no way he intended to act on his desire for Lynn. If the circumstances before had been difficult, now they were impossible.

He gripped the steering wheel more tightly as another flash of lightning rent the blackened skies. It was going to be a short night, for there was no way in hell he was going to let Lynn go out in this storm.

He wasn't allowed to save her if she got into trouble, but he sure as hell could stop her from finding trouble and with nature about to vent its fury, the last place she needed to be was in that shipyard.

Lynn stood at the window and watched the lightning tear across the black sky. The booming thunder rattled the window in its pane.

Although the rain hadn't begun yet, no men stood in front of the tavern. It was not a night for man or beast to be out. A tropical storm warning was in effect for the Miami and surrounding area. Thankfully, it was just a tropical storm and not a full-blown hurricane.

She turned away from the window and sat at the table, waiting for Nick to arrive. It might not be a night for man or beast, but she had a job to do. Hopefully there had been only a few containers unloaded that day and she could get them checked and get back here before the rain began.

She jumped as another crack of thunder boomed overhead. She'd been on edge all day, filled with a restlessness that nothing seemed to dispel.

The days seemed to be getting longer. She hadn't seen Tiny since four days ago when he'd brought over the coffee cake and she'd certainly not had any visitors other than Nick's.

He'd arrive, they'd speak for a few minutes, then she'd take off for the shipyard. The minute she got back to the apartment he took off for whatever life he was living.

As another clap of thunder resounded overhead she checked her wristwatch. Nick should be arriving anytime and tonight, for the first time since they'd begun this job, she wasn't particularly looking forward to seeing him. In fact, if she thought about it for more than a minute she would acknowledge that she was in a pissy mood.

And it was all Nick's fault. The mixed signals she got from him made her mad. The fact that he managed to maintain an emotional distance from her both broke her heart and made her want to shake him.

All day long she'd thought of nothing more than getting out of here and returning to her life in Phoenix. She yearned for her apartment, her routine and her friends.

At some point over the past two days she'd come to the realization that Nick didn't want any kind of a relationship from her other than a working one. She'd lived without him for the past year and she could live without him for the rest of her life.

This morning had started off badly. The coffee-pot had malfunctioned, spilling tepid water all over the countertop. She'd made no further progress with the Spider files. And if that wasn't bad enough, she'd gotten a disturbing e-mail.

As she waited for Nick to arrive she punched on her laptop and pulled up e-mail. She'd checked the message at least ten times during the day as if to assure herself that it hadn't been a figment of her imagination.

There it was, just as it had been the other times she'd checked. She opened the file and stared at the message, a faint chill creeping up her spine.

The top half of the message was a simple spider-web design with a big, black spider in the middle. The text was only one line.

Come into my parlor said the spider to the Athena fly.

It was signed, A.

Even though she had seen the message half a dozen times, it still sent creepy crawlers up her back.

Whoever "A" was, he or she seemed to angry with the Athenas. Inviting a fly into a spiderweb was inviting the fly to die.

What bothered her more than anything was that an enemy of Athena Academy must know that she was working on decoding the Spider files. How?

Lynn had forwarded the e-mail to Delphi, then had spent a couple of hours trying to trace the e-mail address the note had come from. She'd had no success and had instead turned her attention back to the files. But, the message had haunted her throughout the day.

She'd just shut down her computer when she heard Nick's knock under another drumbeat of thunder. She opened the door and as usual he swept past her and to the table, although he didn't sit. He carried with him the familiar duffel bag, which he placed on a chair but didn't open.

"You aren't going out in this." There was an authoritative ring to his words that instantly set her teeth on edge.

She'd already had a crappy day, she didn't need attitude from him. Besides, who in the hell did he think he was to tell her what she was or wasn't going to do?

"Don't be ridiculous," she scoffed and tried to hang on to her temper. After all, it wasn't his fault she'd had a bad day. "I have a job to do and I certainly don't melt in the rain. It's not a hurricane warning, it's just a tropical storm."

He sighed and raked a hand through his thick dark hair. "Lynn, I've had a bad day and I'm not in the mood to argue with you." Stress lines etched down the sides of his face and she could feel the energy that rolled off him.

"Then don't argue with me," she countered. "Maybe I had a bad day, too, but that doesn't mean I don't do my job. How many containers came in today?"

"It doesn't matter." The muscle in his jaw ticked. "You aren't going to clear them tonight." His eyes gleamed darkly and he straightened his shoulders as if spoiling for a fight.

He'd certainly come to the right place, for God knew she was spoiling for one. She'd been tense since the moment she'd arrived back in Miami and suddenly that tension was on the verge of a major explosion.

She took a step toward him. "Have you forgotten? You're just tech support on this assignment. Nobody suddenly died and made you boss."

His eyes narrowed to dark, dangerous slits and he took a step toward her, bringing him close enough that she could smell the scent of the approaching storm, the tang of his cologne, and the underlying whisper of cigarette smoke.

"You're right. I'm nothing more than tech support and certainly not your boss. But, you can't go out there tonight, Lynn. You have to be smart about this. The lightning is almost constant and it will make you a visible target for any guard with a gun."

She knew he was right, but she was feeling reckless, wild. "I can run fast enough that nobody will see me despite the lightning." She turned and headed for the door.

He grabbed her by the arm and twirled her back

around to face him. For a long moment they froze
and when the moment broke, his eyes shone with a
depth of torment just before his mouth crashed to
hers.

Chapter 10

Lynn had waited over a year to taste his kiss again and the moment his mouth took hers, she wrapped her arms around his neck and held tight.

The mouth that had looked so harsh, so grim moments before was now achingly soft and tender as it plied hers with heat.

But it didn't stay soft. With a moan he deepened the kiss, wrapping his arms around her waist as his tongue explored her mouth.

Almost instantly a trembling swept over her body, a want so intense it nearly buckled her knees. It had been so long, so very long since she'd tasted him and felt his body pressed against her own.

She didn't care about containers or storms, she didn't care about promises or tomorrows. All she wanted was this moment in time with this man.

Their tongues swirled together in a wicked dance and their bodies were so close she could feel that he was already fully aroused. The thought that he wanted her as much as she wanted him only stoked her desire higher…hotter.

He tore his mouth from hers, the torment still in his eyes, making them appear darker and more deep-set than usual. "Lynn…we can't…" Despite the words, he made no move to physically distance himself from her. His breath was hot on her face, his hands still gripping her waist.

"Yes we can," she replied and touched her lips to the underside of his throat as she molded her body more tightly against his. She was determined to get what she wanted and what she wanted was to make love with him.

"It's a stormy night and I'm not going anywhere and we have three hours before you have to leave." She spoke with her lips against his collarbone then used her teeth to nibble his skin.

He groaned, as if he found her touch almost painful. Once again she felt conflicting emotions coming from him. Although he didn't stop her, didn't try to escape her, he remained frozen in place.

She raised her head to look at him and saw the conflict on his face. His eyes radiated a fire that threatened to consume her, but his lips pressed tightly together in an expression of faint rebellion. As she continued to stare at him his lips softened, then parted.

If she gave him a moment to think, he'd leave. If she didn't act fast then she knew he'd be lost to her. And she wasn't about to let that happen.

She stepped back from him and pulled her hoodie over her head and dropped it to the floor, leaving the top half of her clad only in a wispy black bra.

He remained not moving, except for his gaze, which swept down to her breasts. Instantly her nipples hardened as if he'd touched her with his hand rather than just with his heated look.

"Make love to me, Nick," she whispered. She reached behind her to unfasten her bra. Before she could manage the hooks, he cursed, then took a step forward and wrapped her in his arms.

Once again his mouth crashed to hers in a kiss that both punished and delighted. His hands stroked the bare skin of her back, then slid downward to cup her buttocks.

It was as if the storm had entered the room. Wild energy coursed through her and the lightning outside the window had nothing on the electricity that sizzled through her veins.

She could feel his heartbeat crashing against her own as he tore his lips from hers and instead trailed kisses down the side of her neck. Hot and hungry, the touch of his mouth made her hum with sweet anticipation.

He pulled her hips against his, grinding against her in frantic rhythm and building the intensity of her desire. She'd forgotten the delicious sensation of hard male against her. But as they rocked together, she remembered and wanted.

Not wanting it to end before they'd even begun, she stepped back and plucked at the bottom of his T-shirt, needing it off, needing to feel the heat of his naked body against hers.

In his eyes she saw a hungry urgency, an urgency she felt, as well. The storm seemed to be on top of them, booming thunder and flashing lightning, but she was lost in Nick's deep brown eyes.

With a groan, he stumbled backward, his eyes blazing and pulled his T-shirt over his head. Thank God she hadn't taken the time that day to make her bed, for she had a feeling if she'd now had to take the time to pull it out, she would have lost him.

Instead, as he dropped his T-shirt to the floor, she took off her bra, then peeled away the black Lycra pants, leaving her clad only in a black thong.

She shut off the light, leaving the room illuminated only by the spill of the light from the bathroom, then she lay down on the bed. Nick reached for the fastening of his jeans. His hands trembled and Lynn embraced the fact that his urgency was obviously as great as her own and she was so hungry for him she thought she might die from it.

He kicked off his shoes and took off his jeans, his

gaze never leaving her. Wearing only socks and briefs, he joined her on the bed.

There was nothing soft or gentle between them. As the storm raged outside and rain began to pound against the window, they became a tangle of arms and legs.

Mouths met in frantic kisses and within mere minutes both her thong and his briefs were gone, cast to the floor with their other clothing.

There was no time, no need for any further foreplay. He moved between her legs and she was wet and ready for him. He pushed deep inside her, then froze and squeezed his eyes tightly shut as his breaths came in short labored pants.

He opened his eyes and stared down at her. "This is going to be too fast." His voice sounded half-strangled. "It's been too long for me."

"It's been as long for me," she replied, her voice sounding as strained as his.

He drew a deep, shuddering breath then shifted his hips against hers. She gripped his sinewy shoulder muscles and arched up to meet him as need clawed at her insides.

He stroked into her fast and furious and she met him thrust for thrust as the rolling tides of her climax came closer and closer.

Lightning flashed and in the glare she saw the tautness of his features, the wildness in his eyes. She cried out as the tides rolled over her, through her. He didn't slow his pace, but rather drove into her with a frenzy that made her climax feel as if it lasted forever.

Then he was there with her, stiffening with a guttural groan that made her want to do it all again. He collapsed on top of her, his heartbeat crashing with her own.

She squeezed her eyes tightly closed as her hand stroked the warm, solid muscle of his back. She loved the feel of his slightly moist, firm skin.

All the tension, all the restlessness that had plagued her for the last couple of days was gone. All she felt at the moment was the sweetness of his body against hers, the faint stir of his breath against her hair and a peace that had been absent for too long.

It had been as good as she remembered. Their bodies had moved together in perfect unison, as if made specifically for one another.

He rolled to the side of her and onto his back. "We didn't use a condom."

"Believe me, a condom was the last thing on my mind," she said dryly. "Besides, I'm on the pill and I haven't been with anyone since I was with you."

As her heartbeat slowed to a more normal pace, she realized she wanted him again. And again. And again.

She had no idea what tomorrow would bring, didn't even know if she would live through the next day. The only thing she knew for certain was that once more with him hadn't been enough.

She got out of bed and went into the bathroom and when she returned, she got back into the bed and turned on her side to face him.

Reaching out to stroke the springy tuft of hair in the center of his chest, she sighed. "I want you again," she whispered. "And this time I want it slow."

He raised a dark eyebrow and released a small laugh. "I'm not a teenager, Lynn."

She smiled and ran her hand lower across the flat of his abdomen. His muscles tensed beneath her caress. "I can make you feel like a teenager."

Once again he laughed, this time sounding half-breathless. He grabbed her hand and held it tight. "You have no idea what you do to me."

"I know what you do to me and I want you to do it to me again now."

He pulled her across his body and met her lips in a kiss of infinite tenderness. It was exactly what she needed after the tumultuous lovemaking they'd just shared.

As he kissed her, his hand smoothed down the length of her back, sending shiver bumps up her spine. She loved the male scent of him, the smell of hot sex that lingered in the air. She loved the way his finger pads felt as they razed across her naked skin and she loved the way his skin felt beneath her own fingertips.

He broke the kiss and instead took one of her nipples into his mouth. The intimate contact shot an electrical current from her breast to the center of her being.

"Apparently you do make me feel like a teen-ager," he said and she realized he was fully aroused once again.

This time she didn't leave it to him to set the pace, rather she straddled him so she could be the one in control. Their lovemaking was slow and languid as they took the time to explore each other.

When they were finished they remained side-by-side, waiting for heartbeats to slow. She wished he could stay all night, wished she could wake up in his arms in the morning.

As he toyed with a strand of her hair she closed her eyes. She'd thought she could make this all about sex and nothing more, that she could embrace the physical release and not be touched on any other level. But she'd been wrong.

Nick had crawled deep into her heart a year ago and nothing had changed for her in that time. He was still as firmly entrenched as ever.

But, she would ask nothing more from him than this. Even though they had just shared mind-blowing lovemaking, she couldn't forget that he'd put up a wall since they'd reunited, a wall that kept him emotionally separated from her.

She had no idea why it was there or if it would ever fall away, but she couldn't force it away with her sheer will.

"You've changed," he finally said softly.

She raised up and looked at him, his features visible in the faint glow from the bathroom light. She considered his words. "Maybe a little. I know I'm stronger than I've ever been. If anything, it isn't that I've changed so much as I've grown up."

It was true. The last year had been one of self-discovery and what she had discovered about herself was that she was strong and capable, that she liked the woman she had become.

"When I was living with Uncle Jonas, he didn't want me to grow up, to be independent or to have a mind of my own. It was in his best interest to keep me weak and dependent on him."

"There's nothing weak or dependent about you now," he replied.

"When did you take up smoking?" she asked.

"What makes you think I smoke?" he countered.

She laid her head back on his chest and twined her fingers in his tuft of hair. "You can't fool me, Nick Barnes. You know I have a terrific sense of smell and several times when you've come in I've smelled cigarette smoke."

"I took it up a couple of months ago...it's a nasty habit."

"Nasty habits should be broken," she said softly.

"When this is over, when everything is over, I'll quit." He ran a finger down her cheek. "Lynn?"

She raised up once again and looked at him. He frowned, a deep cleft shooting across his forehead. "What is it, Nick?" He held her gaze for a long moment, then glanced sideways and she knew he was checking the clock on the end table.

She followed his gaze and saw that the luminous hands read 2:30 a.m. The second bout of leisurely lovemaking had taken longer than she'd thought.

She dreaded the time he would leave, but knew within minutes he'd get up, get dressed and get out. Rain still pelted against the windowpane and the wind howled a mournful tune.

She knew this was probably a one-shot deal, that they wouldn't have the luxury of three hours and a tropical storm to make this happen again.

"I know," she said with a sigh. "It's time for you to go. How many containers came off today?" she asked, wondering how many extra she'd have to clear the next night.

"Only four. You shouldn't have any problems getting to all of them tomorrow night." He sat up and rubbed a hand through his tousled hair. It was as if her question had pulled him away from her. "And you're right. It's time for me to go."

She nodded and watched as he grabbed his clothes from the floor then disappeared into the bathroom. As he closed the door she turned her head into the pillow, smelling the scent of him that lingered there.

He thought she'd changed, but as far as she was concerned, he was the one who was drastically different. The Nick she had known before had been far more open.

The man she'd just made love with had tasted like Nick, had felt like Nick, but when she looked into his eyes, she saw a stranger.

She got out of the bed and turned on the light next to the sofa, then grabbed her robe from the closet and pulled it around her.

As she waited for Nick to come out of the bathroom, she moved to the window and stared out at the rain-soaked streets below. She frowned as she saw a big figure in a black raincoat run from her building and to a big Buick that was always parked in the same spot directly in front of the apartments.

Just before he opened the driver's side door a flash of lightning lit up the sky and in that instant she saw that it was Tiny.

He got into the car and drove off down the street. She frowned thoughtfully. Where would he be going at this time of night? Maybe there was more to the ex-con turned reverend than she'd initially thought.

She turned from the window as Nick came out of the bathroom. "You're going to get soaked," she said.

He grinned and for a moment in that boyish gesture he was the Nick she knew, the man she'd fallen in love with so long ago. "Like you told me earlier, I won't melt."

The sweet smile lasted just an instant, then was gone as his lips pressed tightly together and he headed for the door. He wrapped his hand around the doorknob, then turned back to face her. "Lynn...I..." He frowned. "This shouldn't happen again. Tomorrow night will be business as usual." He didn't wait for her reply but instead opened the door and disappeared into the dark hallway.

She heaved a sigh of frustration, then walked over to the door and locked it. She refused to allow Nick Barnes to make her crazy.

As she walked into the bathroom to clean up and change into her nightgown, she thought of what had just transpired between them.

There had been moments during their lovemaking that she could have sworn what she felt emanating from him was the same intense love, the same deep caring that had marked their earlier relationship. And yet he'd been pretty damned dismissive when he'd left.

What was happening with him? Was his distance just a result of whatever job he was working? She wished she could get into his head and discover those secrets.

She crawled back into the bed she'd left and hugged the pillow that smelled of his scent. What was happening with Nick and what in the hell was Tiny doing out in the middle of a storm in the wee hours of the morning?

Nick leaned his head on the steering wheel of his car and squeezed his eyes tightly closed. When he opened his eyes he slammed his palms down hard against the steering wheel.

Damn. Damn it to hell. He'd just made a terrible mistake. In fact, he hadn't made the mistake once, but twice.

Jesus, he'd been like a drug addict offered a rock of cocaine, unable to stop himself from indulging in something he knew nothing good could come of.

He'd been so filled with resolve where she was

concerned, so certain that he could stand strong. But her temptation had proven stronger than his determination.

The minute she'd kissed the underside of his jaw, the moment that she'd pulled off that hoodie and stood in front of him so proud and beautiful, he'd been lost.

Being with her again had been better than his memories, better than any of the fantasies he'd entertained in the past year. It wasn't just her body that turned him on, although when he'd seen her standing there in just that little black thong he'd nearly come undone without even having to touch her.

No, it wasn't just a physical desire he felt for her. He loved the sound of her laughter, the keen intelligence that shone from her eyes. He liked the way she talked, the way she walked and the way she smelled. She was the only woman who had ever touched his heart.

And she was going to hate him as she'd never hated any other man.

He'd messed up. He'd messed up badly. And nothing good could come from what had just happened.

With a sigh he raised his head and stared through the rain-slick windshield up at her apartment window. It was dark now. Too late for him to go back up and try to explain. He had to get back to his life in Raymore.

Somehow, someway he'd figure out how to get back here tomorrow. First thing in the morning he'd come back and explain to her and somehow make her understand.

He felt sick with self-loathing. He'd always been a strong man. But Lynn made him weak.

He started the engine, then slowly reached into the ashtray and pulled out the solid gold wedding band and slipped in on his finger.

It was time to get back to his wife in Raymore.

Chapter 11

The storm had blown itself out overnight and by ten the next morning the sun was shining brightly and the only sign that there had been a storm was the trash and debris that littered the streets.

Lynn slept late, exhausted after the physical release she'd shared with Nick. When she finally awakened she lounged in the bed, remembering each and every one of his caresses and the wild sensations he'd evoked in her.

When she got up, she showered and dressed, then a glance in the refrigerator let her know a trip to the store was in order. Besides, she wanted to buy a couple more steaks for the devil dogs before tonight's work.

She'd just stepped out into the hallway when she met Tiny getting off the elevator. "Good morning, Lynn." He gave her a tired smile. He filled up the narrow hallway, blocking her path to the exit.

"Good morning, Tiny. You're up and out early considering you were out in the wee hours in the morning."

He frowned, the gesture making him look fierce, almost menacing. "What are you doing, spying on me?"

She forced a light laugh. "Of course not. I was just having that insomnia thing last night and I happened to glance out my window and saw you get into your car around three this morning."

"Trouble don't know what time it is. One of my flock needed me."

"It was a terrible night to have to get out. I guess it was the storm that made it difficult for me to sleep. You look tired."

His frown was replaced by a weary smile. "I'm totally beat. I'm planning on a nice long nap." He pulled his apartment keys out of his pocket.

"I'm off to Pepper's. Do you need anything?" she asked.

His smile widened. "No, but thanks for asking. That's real nice." He moved to the side of the hall so she could slide by him.

"Okay, then. I'll see you later." As she got on the elevator Tiny disappeared into his apartment.

She wondered if he'd told her the truth, if it had

been a member of his flock who had called him out at three in the morning, or if it had been something much different.

She wondered about jailhouse converts, wondered if a sudden finding of faith was often a tool to obtain a Get Out of Jail Free card or if the embracing of good was usually real. Certainly she'd heard that parole boards looked favorably on criminals who repented past sins and vowed to live differently in the future.

The verdict still hung in the balance where Tiny was concerned. For all she knew, his church could be a front for something quite different from praising God.

Dismissing thoughts of her neighbor as she left the building, she breathed in the air, which this morning smelled less of fish and rot and instead held the faint, sweet scent of rain.

It was the third week of September. Although Blake had told her this job would last a week, two at the most, she wasn't surprised that she was still here.

As she walked the block to Pepper's her thoughts once again turned to Nick. A flush of heat swept through her.

Even though he seemed distant most of the time, there had been no distance in those hours they had spent in her bed. His kisses had tasted of a depth of longing that had filled her heart with joy. His loving gaze had given her hope, hope that somehow there was a future waiting for the two of them to share together.

She'd never been one of those women who felt as if she needed a man to complete her. She was just fine on her own.

But she was at a place where she'd love to share her life with somebody special. And last night had only confirmed to her that Nick was her somebody special.

Still, there was no way she could pursue her future with anyone until this job was done. Last night had been a respite from the danger, a magnificent escape from reality. And as Nick had reminded her as he'd walked out of the door, tonight would be business as usual.

Pepper's was a small neighborhood grocery store that carried a vast array of Cuban food. A tiny bell tinkled as Lynn walked in and her mouth instantly watered at the pungent scents that filled the store.

"Welcome." The owner, an older Hispanic man, greeted her with a wide smile. He stood behind an old-fashioned cash register, a woman Lynn guessed was his wife beside him.

"You must be new to the neighborhood," the woman said, her thick Spanish accent evoking in Lynn a homesickness for the couple who had helped to raise her when she'd lived with her Jonas.

"I am," Lynn said. "It's my second time here."

"I am Juan and this is my wife, Mary." The man gestured with a broad sweep of his hands. "If you don't see what you need, just ask."

As Lynn filled her small basket and visited with

the two, her homesickness for Jorge and Rita Batista intensified. The couple, refugees from Cuba, had worked for Jonas and had been as close to parents as Lynn had while growing up. Whenever Jonas traveled, which had been frequently, it had been the plump Rita who had tucked her into bed and sung her Cuban lullabies.

It had been Jorge who had let her watch him clip roses and bushes and had talked to her about nature and birds and anything else she'd wanted to talk about.

When Jonas had fled and his possessions had been seized, Rita and Jorge had been left jobless. It had taken Lynn a month after she'd moved to Phoenix to finally locate them in a small retirement community in Southern California. They had moved there to be close to one of their sons.

She tried to talk to them by phone at least once a month. They never mentioned Jonas's name and neither did Lynn. They always seemed to be pleased when she called and she loved listening to them talk about their children and grandchildren and the fine life they had.

It didn't take her long to gather up and pay for the items she needed. Then, armed with a plastic bag of her purchases, she left the store.

The late-September sun was warm on her shoulders as she walked at a leisurely pace back to her apartment building.

Her thoughts returned to Nick. If there was to be any hope for a future between them, changes would have to be made. There was no way they could make a long-distance relationship work. Been there, done that and it had failed miserably.

People who loved each other weren't meant to live with hundreds or thousands of miles between them. Phone calls and e-mails couldn't fill the void of a lover's absence.

Although she knew she was jumping too far ahead, she couldn't help but wonder what might happen if she and Nick continued their relationship.

It made sense that she would move back to Miami. He'd always worked out of the Florida area and her work was mobile. As long as she had her laptop, she could build Web pages anywhere.

Still, the thought of leaving Phoenix pained her. In the past year she hadn't just built a life there, she'd put down roots. She loved living close to Athena Academy, where the ghost of her mother seemed to linger and comfort her.

It would be difficult to say goodbye to the friends she'd made there, to the community of women who had embraced and welcomed her into their midst. She'd had no close friends when she'd lived with her godfather, just casual college friends. Jonas had discouraged her from making strong bonds with anyone.

She shifted her bag from one arm to the other and frowned as she thought about her friends and Athena Academy. What exactly did that cryptic e-mail mean? Lynn would do anything to protect her

Athena friends from harm. But, how did you fight an enemy you didn't know? She hoped that, whoever Delphi was, she or he was on top of the e-mail and the nebulous threat.

As her apartment building came into view, Lynn's heart leaped in pleasant surprise. Sitting on the steps with the sun shining in his dark hair was Nick.

He didn't see her and she took a moment to drink in the sight of him. Even in worn jeans and a T-shirt, with his hair too long and whiskers shadowing his jaw, he was an intensely handsome man.

Just looking at him swept a rush of lust through her and she wondered if it would always be that way. Would she always feel a thrill when she looked at him? Would he always make her heart beat just a little faster? Somehow she thought so.

What was he doing here in the middle of the day? As he turned his head in her direction she waved and hurried toward him, unable to stop the rush of joy that suffused her. But, the joy was short-lived as she saw the grim expression on his face.

Something had happened. Had he been pulled off her operation? Had he come to tell her another agent would be taking over?

He stood as she approached. No smile curved his lips as he looked at her. "We need to talk."

Whatever it was, it was bad. She knew how bad it was by how fast the muscle in his jaw ticked. She dropped her bag to the sidewalk and reached up to place a hand against that taut, muscled jaw. She couldn't help herself. She needed to touch him. "What's wrong, Nick?"

He was silent for a long minute as he placed his hand over hers. His dark eyes radiated an emotion deeper than torment, an emotion that banked and dived into a chasm of anguish.

"Nick, please talk to me. You're scaring me," she said softly.

"Hey, Nicky." The deep voice came from a man coming across the street toward them. His blond hair glistened in the sun and his wide-open features wore a friendly smile.

Nick dropped his hand from hers and she stepped back from him. If he'd radiated tension before, it was nothing compared to what she now felt pulsing from him. Who was this man who filled Nick with such stress?

"Jimmy," Nick said in obvious surprise. "What are you doing here?"

The man named Jimmy grinned, a sly grin as his gaze swept over her, then back to Nick. "I'd say the question isn't what I'm doing here, but rather does your wife know what *you're* doing here?"

Lynn's heart seemed to stop beating as the world tilted on its axis. Wife? Nick was *married?* In a flash a million thoughts tumbled through her head. The secrets she'd sensed in him, the emotional distance that had existed between them. Was that why he only had three hours a night to spend with her?

He was married.

A roar filled her ears as she stared at him. She wanted him to deny it, but the truth was in his eyes. Unaware of her own intention, she slapped him. Hard. Hard enough that she felt the impact not only in her hand, but clear up into her shoulder.

"Jesus," the man named Jimmy exclaimed.

"Lynn." His voice was a groveling appeal. He reached out to her, but she stumbled backward, away from him. She needed to get away. She had to escape from him and his lies.

A sob broke loose from someplace deep inside her and she turned and ran. She was vaguely aware of him calling her name once again and heard the sound of his footsteps as he started after her.

He'd never catch her. She was faster than any man. She raised her head, breathed through her nose and ran as fast as she'd ever run in her life.

But no matter how fast she ran she knew there was no way she could outrun the pain of his betrayal.

Nick ran a block before he realized he'd never be able to catch up with her. His cheek burned with pain, but it was nothing compared to the ache in his heart and the heaviness of fear that knotted his stomach.

Jimmy. What in the hell was he doing here? As he turned around to go back to the apartment building he saw Jimmy standing on the sidewalk.

He'd have to deal with Lynn later. Hopefully someway he'd figure out how to make this right. At the moment, he had to make sure that his cover was safe, that Jimmy's presence here wasn't the prelude to a bullet through his brain.

As he approached, Jimmy held out his hands as if in supplication. "Jesus, man. I'm sorry. She didn't know you were married?"

"I usually don't make a habit of telling my girlfriend that I have a wife. It's about as smart as telling your wife you have a mistress."

Nick shoved his hands in his pockets and gave Jimmy a look of disgust. "Thanks a lot, man. You probably just screwed me up royally." His heart crashed against his ribs in a controlled panic. He still didn't know why Jimmy was here or what he might know.

Jimmy shook his head and cast him a look of approval. "I got to hand it to you, Nicky. That was one hot-looking broad. You said her name was Lynn?"

Nick nodded and his mind raced. "Lynn White. She's Jonas White's goddaughter. I met her when I was working for him and we've been kicking it ever since."

He decided to tell the truth about who she was, afraid to lie because he was unsure of what resources they might have to learn the truth.

He looked at Jimmy with a sheepish grin. "You know I love your cousin and I'm totally committed to her and the marriage, but Colette's just not into sex much."

"And why not have your cake and eat it, too," Jimmy

said. "Hey man, I don't blame you. I always figured my cousin was more than a little bit of a prude."

Nick forced a laugh. "You've got that right. She's a lights out, everything under the covers kind of a woman."

Jimmy snickered. "I'll bet she thinks oral sex means sex with a piece of gum in your mouth."

Nick laughed, although his gut remained twisted in a tight knot. "So, what are you doing here, Jimmy? Spying on me? Did Colette put you up to this?" He knew Colette would never be behind Jimmy's presence here.

"Yeah, I'm spying on you, but not for Colette."

Nick raised an eyebrow, surprised by Jimmy's answer, surprised that he'd admitted that he was spying. Once again his heartbeat raced with dread. "You want to tell me what's going on?"

Jimmy shrugged. "I got a call yesterday morning from the man. He said it had come to his attention that you were making nightly runs to a destination unknown. He told me he wanted me to follow you and find out what was going on. I was just doing what I was told to do."

Dammit. Nick's stomach muscles clenched even tighter. Who had seen him coming and going from his house in the middle of the night? Who had been watching him and why hadn't he noticed? Had he compromised the operation in Raymore by not being careful enough?

"So, last night I followed you here and saw you

go inside." Jimmy grinned slyly. "It must have been a good night. You were in there for quite a while."

Nick returned the grin. "One of the best. She's always crazy during a storm. She was wild, hot as a pistol and ready to pop." He hated talking about Lynn in such derogatory terms, but he had no choice. Jimmy had to believe that Lynn was nothing more than a hot piece on the side that brought Nick out each night.

"Anyway, when you left your place this morning, I followed you again and here we are. I think the man was worried that maybe you weren't as committed to our project as he thought you were."

"Put me in tough with him, Jimmy. I'll talk to him. The only betrayal I got on my mind is a little marital infidelity. I don't want there to be any doubts about my commitment to what we're all doing."

Jimmy kicked at a piece of trash on the sidewalk. "Wish I could accommodate you, but he calls me. I don't even know his name."

"You've got to have some idea. Hell, you're the *only* one who talks to him." Nick's frustration threatened to unleash and he quickly tamped it down.

Jimmy shook his head and gazed at Nick earnestly. "I swear I don't have a clue. When he calls me he uses one of those computer voice things. It makes him sound like a freakin' alien. I could be talking to my own mother and wouldn't recognize her voice. But, trust me, I'll pass on the information that we've got nothing to worry about. What you need to worry about is Colette finding out what you've been up to. She finds out she'll shave your balls and hang them out like walnuts on the nearest tree."

"Then I guess my balls are in your court," Nick replied. He stared at Jimmy, trying to see if there was any hint of suspicion in his eyes, but Jimmy's gaze gave nothing away.

"Ah, don't worry. I'm not about to tell Colette. Whatever happens in your marriage is none of my business." Jimmy clapped him on the back and grinned widely. "Your secret is safe with me. I just hope my big mouth didn't screw things up with you and your hot little honey."

"I'll just have to do some fast-talking to make things right," Nick replied. "You know women. I'll buy her a little piece of jewelry and she'll come around."

"I got to get back to Raymore and report in. I'll see you back there."

Nick watched as Jimmy walked away. The knot in his stomach had eased somewhat. He thought Jimmy had bought his story and Nick's cover was safe.

Where had Lynn gone? His chest ached as he thought of the look that had swept over her face when she'd learned he was married. He'd never forget that stark look of utter horror, the pale torment of one betrayed. For the second time.

He needed to explain to her the circumstances of his marriage. He wanted her to understand that it had all been part of his undercover work. The woman he was *married* to knew where he went each night and all about his work with Lynn.

Lowering himself to the stoop in front of her building, he rubbed his cheek, where the force of her slap still stung. He wondered how long it would be before she returned to the apartment. More important he wondered what he could possibly do to make this right.

Chapter 12

Lynn ran until she couldn't run any farther, half-blind with tears as she cursed Nick, then cursed herself. When her ribs ached and her chest burned, she finally collapsed on a bus stop bench.

Married.

He was *married*.

The words echoed with horror through her brain. He had a wife. Lynn had been a cat burglar, she'd done some terrible things in her past because of her godfather's influence, but that didn't mean she didn't adhere to a strict moral code, a code that didn't make it okay to sleep with a married man.

She would have never slept with him had she

known. It was a major taboo as far as she was concerned. How could he have done this? He'd betrayed not only her, but another woman, as well. His *wife*.

She squeezed her eyes closed against a new flood of tears. What had he been thinking? How had he been able to justify allowing them to make love?

Now she certainly understood the emotional distance she'd felt from him, the secrets that had darkened his eyes. Men who screwed around on their wives kept secrets. Men who cheated on their wives were only available for their mistresses part of the time.

A fool. She'd been such a stupid fool. Even though she thought she could have sex with him and not get emotionally involved, she'd been wrong.

She'd been entertaining fantasies of marrying him, building a life with him and having his children. She'd dreamed of traditions and a normal life, and she'd wanted it all with him.

"Stupid fool," she muttered as she watched a gull pick at a discarded sandwich wrapper nearby. She should have listened to her instincts, she should have recognized that something wasn't right. But, she'd been so bent on getting what she wanted, what she desired.

Well, she'd gotten it. She'd made love to him one last time and the cost of her pleasure was a broken heart, broken trust and broken dreams.

Although the bench was hard against her butt and the sun grew uncomfortably warm, she remained sitting there throughout the afternoon.

She was afraid to go back, afraid that he would be waiting for her and she didn't want to look at him, didn't want to talk to him right now. He'd come back to the apartment tonight because he was assigned to do so. She'd face him then.

His betrayal of her hurt, but the pain was particularly intense because he was the one man in her life she'd trusted. She'd trusted him to be straight with her, to never lie to her again. Dammit, he'd known what Jonas's lies had done to her.

Throughout the afternoon people came and went, getting on and off the buses that stopped occasionally at the corner. She sat, her anger, her pain slowly transforming to numbness.

She listened to the women who passed by talk about what they were fixing for dinner and how their children were doing in school. Men talked of the upcoming Miami Dolphin football game and household chores. She envied all of them for their normal lives.

It was just after dusk when she finally roused herself from the bench and started the long walk back to her apartment building.

She'd run a long way from her apartment and it took her several moments to get her bearings to know which direction to walk home.

As she started walking she realized that in those hours of sitting on that bench, she'd found her strength once again. She didn't need him in her life. She was fine alone.

There would be no more tears for Nick Barnes. No

man would ever make her cry again. When this assignment was all over she'd go back to her life in Phoenix,
maybe get drunk and stupid and go to bed with Leo.

And tonight when Nick showed up at the apartment, they would be nothing more than two people
working for the government for the common good.
She didn't want to hear explanations or excuses from
him. Nothing could explain or excuse the fact that
he was married and had slept with her anyway.

She was about sixteen blocks from the apartment
building when a familiar dark-colored big Buick
pulled to the curb and honked. She saw Tiny at the
wheel and Stella in the passenger seat.

Stella rolled down her window. "Hey, girl. Do
you need a ride?"

Lynn contemplated the offer as a sudden wave of
sheer exhaustion swept over her. The emotional
burden of the day weighed heavily on her, making
her legs feel like lead. "Are you going to give me any
shit?" she asked the hooker.

Stella grinned and the gesture made her irregular
features almost pretty. "Nah, I'm not in the mood to
get my ass whipped again. Besides, I got my con-
science with me." She stuck her thumb out to indicate
Tiny.

Lynn considered for just a minute, then stepped
off the sidewalk, opened the back door and slid into
the cavernous interior of the old car. It smelled like
stale fast food and some sort of pine air freshener,
but the car was spotlessly clean. "Thanks," she said.

"No problem," Tiny replied. "We were just on our way back from visiting a mutual friend."

"An old boyfriend of mine who's in county lockup," Stella said. She turned around in the seat and looked at Lynn. "You got a boyfriend?"

Lynn's initial impulse was to shout a resounding no, but she didn't know what Tiny and Stella might know. Had they seen Nick coming and going from her apartment in the middle of the night? "Yeah, I've got a boyfriend," she replied. "But, he works weird hours so we don't see much of each other."

Stella eyed her with speculation. "You two have a fight? You look like you're upset."

"Yeah, we had a little fight," Lynn replied.

"Let them get into your pants, but never let them get into your heart, that's what I always say. Me, I got lots of boyfriends," Stella said. "Mostly dockworkers that smell like fish, but they all treat me okay."

That was more than Lynn could say about her "boyfriend." She settled back in the seat as Stella continued to look at her in open curiosity. "So, what did you fight about?"

"Stella, mind your business," Tiny chided.

Stella huffed indignantly. "I am minding my business. I've just decided her business is mine." She smiled at Lynn.

"Tiny told me you do all kinds of computer stuff."

"That's right."

"Maybe you could make him—" she pointed a

thumb at Tony "—one of those Web page things to advertise his church. I hear that's what everyone is doing these days, those Web pages. He's a good preacher but nobody ever comes to the church. I keep telling him nobody knows he's there and he needs to advertise. A Web page would maybe help."

"Stella," Tiny admonished. "That's Lynn's work and you know I don't have any money. That's like her asking you to turn a trick for free."

"I've done that before," Stella protested. "When it's somebody I really like."

"I'll make you a Web page, Tiny," Lynn said as they pulled up in front of the apartment building. It would only take her maybe a half an hour to pull together something simple.

"I can't ask you to do that." He shut off the car engine.

Stella huffed in exasperation. "You're always preaching to ask and you'll receive."

"It's no big deal, Tiny. I can get something up and running sometime tomorrow."

They all got out of the car and Lynn was thankful to see there was no sign of Nick. The groceries she'd bought and had dropped to the sidewalk were gone, as well, probably stolen by one of her neighbors. She hoped they enjoyed the big juicy steaks she'd bought to feed to the dogs in the shipyard.

"Thanks for the ride," she said.

"No problem. Stella and I are going to head down to the church. You want to join us?" Tiny asked.

She shook her head. "Not tonight. I have some things to do."

"Okay then, we'll see you later."

Lynn watched as the two headed down the sidewalk, Stella's skinny hips swinging like a hyper bell. When they'd disappeared from her sight, she turned and stared at the entrance to her apartment building.

She wasn't ready to go back inside. She wasn't ready to face the small confines of the room and the bed that she hadn't made with the sheets and pillow-cases that smelled like Nick.

She suddenly remembered the car that had been provided for her, a car she hadn't touched in the time she'd been here. She pulled the keys from her purse, then walked around the back of the building to the parking lot.

There it was, a beat-up black sedan with the license plate number BAW029. It was a far cry from the sports car she'd driven when she'd been living with Jonas.

She got into it and headed out, away from the dock area. Driving had always been her escape. When she'd been with Jonas, her little sports car had been her best friend. Whenever she was feeling stifled by Jonas's overbearing and overprotective ways, she'd sneak out of the house and into her car and drive.

Although this car didn't have half the power of the vehicle she'd once owned, she pushed it to the max with all the windows open so the evening air could blow in her hair.

A wild abandon filled her as she zoomed by other cars on the road. She'd like to drive forever. Drive away from her heartache, from the job that had her crawling into containers and from anyone who wanted or needed anything from her.

She had enough money in her purse to drive to the state of Washington or Oregon, where she knew nobody and nobody knew her. But, she wouldn't. She'd never been one to run away from problems.

She left behind the dock area and headed down a highway that would take her to the familiar streets she'd once haunted.

She passed an upscale boutique where she'd often shopped for clothes and accessories and drove by a restaurant where she'd often met her college buddies.

She'd lost touch with her friends when she'd moved. Besides, she'd been too embarrassed by the news reports of Jonas's crimes to maintain those friendships. She'd been afraid she'd see pity or curiosity in their eyes and she didn't know which would be worse.

Memories flooded her brain, mostly good memories of a time when she'd been ignorant and relatively happy. She'd been blissfully ignorant of the evil Jonas harbored in his heart. She'd been a college student pursuing a career in computer science and thought she was doing good deeds with the work Jonas gave her. And, for a little while, she'd had Nick.

She frowned and tightened her fingers around the steering wheel. Or had she? Although he'd professed to love her at that time, he'd also had a job to do. In the effort to get close to Jonas, he'd consciously set out to seduce her.

And seduce her he had. She'd fallen for him like a fragile palm tree in a hurricane, tumbled head over heels for his charm, his wit and his passion.

Had it all been nothing more than an illusion? Even though he'd told her afterward that the seduction had been ordered, but had been heartfelt.

He'd assured her that his feelings for her were real and true but in retrospect she didn't know what to believe. After all, he hadn't mentioned the little fact that he was married.

He'd proven himself to be a man who would do anything to get the job done. He was a man committed to his work. He'd been working undercover jobs for so long she wondered if he'd lost touch with who he really was.

Had last night simply been a way to mollify her and keep her happy? She hadn't hidden the fact that she wanted him. Had he decided to give her what she wanted to stop the fight they'd been about to have? Had it merely been a way to win the fight, a way to keep her from going out in the storm?

She pulled the car to a halt in front of a pair of familiar massive gates. She turned off the engine and stared through the ornate security gates and up the driveway to the mansion beyond.

This was the home of her childhood, the place where she had lived in splendor with a man who had never loved her, but had used her. This was the place where she'd been groomed to break the law, where she'd been encouraged to explore her genetic enhancements and use them to gain wealth for Jonas White.

She got out of the car and stood, noticing that there were lights on in various windows of the house. The government had seized the property when they'd gone after Jonas, but apparently since then it had been sold to somebody.

Somebody had used her all her life. As far as she was concerned, Jonas's crimes against her were no greater than those of Nick. Betrayal tasted just as bitter no matter who perpetrated it.

Although she'd had moments of happiness here in this big mansion, she'd never really been happy. She'd longed for an average life. She'd hated the genetic gifts that Jonas told her made her a potential kidnapping victim, forced her to live like a prisoner.

A steely resolve filled her as she got back into her car. She'd finish what she started. She'd do the job at the shipyard and she'd continue to work with Nick, but it would be the last time she'd be used by anyone.

Hell hath no fury like a woman scorned, Nick thought as he rode the elevator up to Lynn's floor that night. He'd only seen Lynn angry once before and that had been the night she'd discovered he wasn't one of Jonas's grunts but was rather an FBI agent.

Her anger had been an awesome force to behold. As he knocked on the apartment door he was prepared for the worst. He was prepared for the possibility that Lynn might very well rip his throat out before he got an opportunity to say anything.

All he wanted was a chance to explain, an opportunity to make her understand the position he was in and why he hadn't told her about his marriage.

But, the woman who opened the door to admit him didn't have fury burning in her eyes. As usual she was clad all in black, ready for the night's work. Instead of the warmth that usually lit her eyes when he walked through the door, her unusual blend of green-and-gold eyes radiated a coldness that was far worse than any anger.

"How many containers?" she asked without preamble.

Nick placed his duffel bag on the table and gazed at her. She looked as beautiful as he'd ever seen her, with her chestnut hair swept up into a ponytail emphasizing the graceful curve of her neck and her delicate features.

"We need to talk," he said.

"No, we don't," she replied tersely. "We have nothing to talk about except how many containers came off the ships tonight."

Her eyes, which had always sparked with such life, with such emotion were dead and their very lifelessness made him mourn. "Lynn, you need to let me explain."

A flash of color swept over her cheeks. "Are you married?"

"Yes, but…"

"Then the discussion is over."

"Dammit, Lynn, you've got to listen to me." He exploded, raising his voice to a near shout. He hit the table loudly with the palm of his hand, driven by a combination of frustration and anger.

She crossed her arms over her chest and glared at him. "You've got some nerve raising your voice to me after what you've done."

As quickly as it had come, the anger left and Nick sank down heavily on one of the chairs at the table. "You're right. I'm sorry." He closed his eyes and rubbed the center of his forehead and wondered how everything had gotten so screwed up.

He opened his eyes once again to see her still standing with her arms defensively crossed, but pain radiating from her eyes. "How could you, Nick? How could you sleep with me knowing that you belong to another woman? How could you do that? How could you lie to me?"

"I never lied," he protested. She narrowed her eyes. "Okay, I lied by omission," he admitted. "I should have told you, I know that."

Her eyes held the faint sheen of emotion, but her features remained passive. Even though he knew he probably couldn't ever make it right, he had to try. He stood and faced her.

"It's not a real marriage, Lynn. It's a legal one, but

it isn't real. It's part of my cover. I needed an in on the assignment I'm working in a small town. The FBI had a contact who was a local woman. The only way to make everyone believe the relationship and get me where I needed to be was to marry Colette. I couldn't tell you because I didn't want to compromise the job in any way."

"And so you compromised me."

He winced. "The marriage is nothing more than a paper legality."

"It's a paper legality that matters," she cried and unfolded her arms.

"I know." Once again he rubbed his forehead and wondered why he hadn't told her. He'd had a week and a half to tell her, but he hadn't. Maybe he hadn't wanted to because he'd known that if he did, last night wouldn't have happened.

If he'd told her he was married she would have made sure that last night didn't happen. The thought that he hadn't told her so she wouldn't stop their lovemaking made him a real selfish bastard.

He stood, wanting nothing more than to take her in his arms, but he knew better than to even attempt it.

"I tried to keep last night from happening. I knew it wasn't the right thing to do, but I'm a weak man where you're concerned, Lynn."

He tore a hand through his hair in frustration. "Dammit, I tried not to get close, not to smell your damned perfume and remember how you felt in my arms. I tried not to want you because I knew I shouldn't have you. But, I screwed up. I let things get way out of control. And once you were in my arms, I couldn't stop."

He thought he saw a softening in her eyes, but it was there only a moment, then gone. "What's done is done," she said. "And now we have work to do."

He knew nothing more he could say to her now would make any difference. She was completely closed off to him. All he could hope for was that before all this was over he'd get an opportunity to talk to her again.

"Eight containers," he said as he handed her the latest photo of the shipyard.

"Plus the ones from last night. I'll see you at three." With those final words she disappeared out the door.

Chapter 13

As Lynn walked toward the shipyard, she tried not to think about Nick or what he'd said. She knew how dangerous it was to work while being distracted.

Still, it was hard not to think about what he'd told her. He'd said the marriage had been part of his undercover work and was only a paper legality.

What he didn't understand was, to her it didn't matter. Married was married and any hope she'd had of any kind of a relationship with him was gone.

How could she believe anything he'd said to her? How did she know that he'd told her the truth, about another assignment, about his marriage? She'd lost all trust in him and that hurt as much as anything.

Even if he had told her the truth, he would always be a man who put the job first, who would make all kinds of personal sacrifices for his work.

Okay, so nothing had really changed in her life except it had now been one night since she'd had good sex rather than over a year. Nick was nothing more than a memory and that's what he would have to remain.

The night was warm and a three-quarter moon shone from a cloudless sky. She would have much preferred dark clouds.

She picked up her pace and shoved thoughts of Nick away. She'd blown off working on the Spider files today but had checked her e-mail when she'd first rolled out of bed.

There had been no further communication from A. But that didn't stop her from being concerned about the first e-mail she'd received. Who knew about her connection with the women and the school? It had to be connected to the Spider files. As soon as she got back to Phoenix, she intended to have another talk with Kim Valenti.

As the shipyard came into view she emptied her mind, focusing only on the job that had to be done. She went over the wall in the same place she had every night. She hit the ground inside the holding area with barely a thud, then froze as she surveyed her surroundings.

In the distance she could hear the sounds of guards talking, but they were far enough away that she wasn't too concerned. Thankfully, she didn't sense the close presence of any dogs.

Still, she wished she had the steaks she'd bought that morning at the store just in case she was to encounter any of the dogs.

"I'm in," she said softly, letting Nick know over the transmitter on the collar of her hoodie. *I'm in, and you're a jerk*, she wanted to say. She'd love to give him a piece of her mind now, while he could hear her and she couldn't hear him.

It was every angry woman's dream, to talk until she was talked out without a man being able to interrupt or make explanations.

Of course she wouldn't do it. Although it would certainly make her feel better to vent all the emotions she had stuffed inside her, she couldn't risk unnecessary chatter that might be overheard by a guard.

Instead, she got to work. Quickly, efficiently she picked the lock on the first container that had to be checked. The door rolled up without so much as a squeak. She slipped inside and used her penlight to view the contents.

The interior was stifling hot. Racks of clothing and crates of shoes were inside. It took her only a few moments to run her scanner over the lot. "Container 15596 cleared," she said as she eased the door down and returned the lock to its place. One down, eleven to go.

For the next hour she moved from container to container, clearing them and letting Nick know the number of each one.

As she snapped the lock on the fifth container of the night, a flashlight shone from around the corner of a nearby container. She hit the ground with enough force to momentarily knock the wind out of her.

She pressed her face against the concrete and tried to make herself as small as possible. Don't find me, she thought. Please don't see me.

"Julie has been bitching that we never do anything, we never go anywhere." The male voice sounded young.

"Wives always bitch about something," a deeper voice replied.

"She doesn't understand that working these hours makes it hard to do the club scene or go to parties."

"Wait until you two have kids, then she'll really have something to bitch about."

Lynn's heart pumped frantically and she pressed herself harder against the concrete on the ground beneath her. If they came around the corner with that flashlight there was no way they'd miss her. She'd be arrested and spend the next fifteen or twenty years in jail.

The last time she'd been arrested, when Nick and his FBI buddies had caught her when she'd been working for Jonas, she'd been locked up and her sister Dawn had broken her out of jail.

Of course, at the time Lynn hadn't known that Dawn existed. Dawn had come into the jail like an avenging angel, setting up a couple of small bombs to provide a distraction while she rescued Lynn.

I should have run then, she thought. I should have claimed a new identity when I had the chance. But she hadn't run. Not wanting to live her life in shadows, always looking over her shoulder, she'd turned herself in to Nick and had agreed to help the FBI take down Jonas.

Dawn wouldn't be around to help her this time and Nick had strict orders not to ride to her rescue. She was on her own, flying without a net.

She felt every gravel pebble beneath her body. The light flashed again. She pressed her cheek into the ground. Winced as the rough concrete abraded the side of her face.

Breathe. She had to focus on taking a breath, then another. Every muscle tensed as she prepared to run. *Go away.* She mentally willed the men to move to another area.

She smelled the scent of sulfur from a lit match, heard the faint draw of breath that indicated to her one of the men had lit a cigarette.

Her entire body trembled with nervous tension. Would they never go away?

She drew her first breath since hitting the ground as the voices finally, mercifully drifted farther away. She remained lying down for several long seconds, then eased into a sitting position.

She winced. Every contact point she'd made with the pavement ached. Thank God they hadn't come around the corner and found her. "That was close," she whispered.

Getting up, she drew a deep breath to steady her nerves, then proceeded to the next container, eager to get the night's work done and get back to the apartment.

With her nervous tension in check, she quickly moved to the next container. Once again it only took her a few seconds to pick the lock, then she eased open the door and stepped inside.

Her penlight showed that it was packed with crates. The packing invoice described the contents as pottery and glassware. The crates were packed from floor to ceiling on either side of a narrow aisle.

Using the hand scanner, she worked her way from front to back, the air quickly becoming stifling as she moved toward the very back of the enclosure.

As she ran the scanner across one of the crates in the very back of the container, it lit up like a Christmas tree. She froze, stunned, and held the scanner out once again. No doubt about it, the reading was clear. Something in one of the crates didn't belong there.

Breathing shallowly, fear suffusing her, she moved closer and saw that on the side of the crate that had lit up the scanner appeared to be a timer of sorts.

Bomb!

She'd found it.

The chatter that Blake and his agency had gotten had been right. There was a bomb.

"Nick, container 16002. The bomb's in here. Contact Blake. Tell him I found the bomb. Container 16002."

Out! She wanted out. She had to get out of here.

Her job was done and all she had to do was get to safety. She backed away from the crate, wondering what kind of timer it was on, when it was set to explode.

For all she knew it could go off before she made her way out of the container. It appeared to be big enough to take out half the wharf.

She turned to exit just in time to hear the sharp bark of a dog. The door of the container crashed down. For a long moment she stared at it in horror. Busted!

She was caught like a rat in a trap.

Inside the container.

She was trapped inside the container with the bomb.

Panic ripped through her.

She had to get out. She had no idea when the bomb was set to detonate. If the choices were life in a prison cell versus being blown to smithereens, she'd take the cell every time.

Working her way down the narrow aisle to the door she tried to lift it, but it didn't budge. Whoever had closed it had apparently secured it, as well.

Think! Think Lynn, she commanded. For a long moment she felt as if she suffered some sort of brain freeze. She couldn't think. She couldn't act. She could do nothing but stare at the door that held her captive.

Frantically she used her penlight to survey the walls of the container, looking for a weakness she could exploit, a way out other than the door. But, there was none.

"Hey! Somebody let me out of here," she cried

and banged on the door with her fists. The pounding of her hands against the metal door sounded muted compared to the frantic beating of her heart.

The walls seemed to close in on her and she was struck by a horrifying wave of claustrophobia. She couldn't breathe. She couldn't get enough air. It was too hot. The walls were too close.

She slid to the floor next to the door and fought back tears of defeat. She couldn't get out. The bomb could go off at any minute and she wouldn't be able to escape.

She was only twenty-three years old and one way or another her life, for all intents and purposes, was over tonight.

It didn't matter that Nick was married and unattainable. If the bomb didn't go off before the door opened, eventually she'd be arrested and nobody would come to help her.

"Nick, I'm in trouble," she said softly. "I'm locked in the container with the bomb and for all I know it could go off at any moment." She fought back a burst of hysterical laughter. Although logically she didn't think it would detonate, she knew that the terrorist probably had plans for the bomb. At the moment, emotions were stronger than logic. "They showed me how to find a bomb, but they didn't teach me how to disarm one."

She leaned her head against the door and was able to hear the sounds of men talking. They were probably trying to decide the best way to handle the situation.

"If I manage to get out of this container, then I'm headed to jail for a very long time. You know all the charges that are pending against me." She drew a deep breath and squeezed her eyes tightly closed as all the moments she'd had with Nick in the past two weeks rushed through her head.

The heat of his kiss, the sweet touch of his hands, all of it swept through her, bringing with it a grief so profound it momentarily stilled her fear. She'd always remember that smile of his. She loved the way he could make her laugh. Whether she lived another twenty years in a jail cell or was blown to bits in minutes, she'd have him in her heart.

She had no idea what the truth was where he was concerned, but it didn't matter now. She'd never see him again. The average, normal life she'd hungered for was never going to happen.

It wasn't fair. She wanted a future. She needed more time, time to get to know her father better, time to be with her sisters and share their lives. She'd wanted children. Dammit, she'd wanted a future.

She bit her lower lip, willing tears away. "Nick, I know you have your orders and I'm on my own here. I just want you to know that I wouldn't take back any of the time we had together."

A tear escaped to run down her cheek and she swiped at it angrily. "Even knowing that you're married, I wouldn't take back making love to you. I love you, Nick. I just wanted you to know that."

She reached up to touch the tiny transmitter on her collar and froze. The transmitter was gone.

Chapter 14

In a new panic, she frantically raked her hand across her neckline, but the tiny bug that had connected her with Nick wasn't anywhere.

A hysterical burst of laughter nearly choked her. She was baring her heart to nobody. He hadn't heard a word she'd said. He didn't know she was in trouble and he didn't know about the bomb.

Alone. Just knowing that Nick could hear her speak, could listen to her final words, had comforted her. Now that comfort had been torn away and she knew she was truly alone.

The transmitter must have fallen off when she'd hit the ground so hard earlier. She must have jarred it loose.

The phone! She fumbled in her pouch for the phone Nick had given her to carry. She flipped it open and in the tiny display saw the words, No Signal.

Once again she bit back a burst of hysterical laughter. Of course there was no signal. Why make things easier on her?

The knowledge that she was truly alone, that Nick couldn't even hear her thoughts, galvanized her. She might be going down, but she wasn't going down easily.

She stood and emptied her pouch. She took out the lock-picking kit and the phone and hid them along with the scanner behind one of the crates. When they got her out of here, she didn't want to be found with those items.

She banged on the door once again. "Hey, come on, let me out," she screamed, certain that they could hear her. "It was just a stupid dare, okay? Come on, don't be a bunch of hard-asses. My friends are waiting for me down at the bar."

It was a gamble, but she figured her best chance of getting out of this whole debacle was to play dumb. If she could just get outside maybe she'd have an opportunity to escape.

"I'm getting really freaked out in here," she yelled. "Please, open the door…I…I can't breathe in here."

"It's a girl," one of the men outside the door said. "It sounds like she's in there by herself." The voice sounded young and she thought it might have been the person who'd been talking about his wife earlier.

"I only saw one person in there when I shut the door," another deep voice replied.

"What do you think, should we open it?" It was the younger-sounding male voice.

"Please, help me. I'm so scared. I'm going to be sick. You gotta let me out of here!" She banged on the door once again and nearly sobbed as she heard the latch on the door turning.

She gathered all the strength she had and stood poised as the door slid up. Her intention had been to spring out of the container and run as she'd never run before. Two guns pointed directly at her changed her mind.

"Oh, thank God," she cried and half collapsed on the ground just outside the container. As she pretended to suck in air and sob, she kept an eye on the two guards, looking for any weakness they might display.

A Doberman stood on either side of the older man, the dogs looking at her as if she were a particularly juicy filet mignon. They vibrated with excitement, their powerful haunches tensed.

"Aufhalten," the man said.

He couldn't know that Lynn's education had been extensive, including learning languages such as German. *Stay,* he'd said and although both dogs whined plaintively, they remained still. She'd heard somewhere that guard dogs were often trained in a foreign language so that most people wouldn't know what commands to give.

"Stand up," he commanded her in English. "Who

are you?" He had no German accent, adding to her speculation that only the dog training had been done in the German language.

She pretended to struggle to her feet, her arms clenched around her stomach as if she might throw up at any moment. "My name is Lynn and this was all a stupid bet with my friends. We had a couple of drinks and one of the guys came up with this stupid idea."

"You bunch of idiots," the younger man exclaimed. "What were you thinking?"

"I don't know. Oh God, oh God, my parents are going to totally kill me." She boo-hooed like a baby, wailing loudly and watched slyly as the two men exchanged uneasy glances.

"Okay…all right. Calm down for crying out loud," the older man said and lowered his weapon. "You can tell it all to our supervisor when he gets here."

The younger guard lowered his weapon, as well. It was all Lynn had been waiting for. She sprang, kicking straight out and knocked the gun out of the older man's hand, then she spun and roundhouse kicked the other gun.

"Angreifen! Angreifen!" The older guard yelled, then cursed soundly.

Attack!

The dogs leaped forward as Lynn took off running. She knew she had only seconds before the guards would recover their weapons and less time before one of those dogs would make her his next meal.

She darted around the corner of one row of containers, then around another. She would have felt better if the dogs barked and growled, but they were ominously silent as they chased after her.

She skidded around another corner, gasping as she nearly fell. If she tripped, if she stumbled and fell, she would be finished. The dogs would be on her like diamonds on a debutante.

All she needed was enough time to get out of the holding enclosure. At the moment she felt like a sitting duck, waiting for the bite of sharp teeth or the sting of a bullet in her back.

The guards yelled to each other and it was easy to tell from their voices that they were furious. If they caught her they wouldn't fall for her poor little girl act again.

She was in the center of the yard and the containers formed a maze. She kept her gaze focused on the distant wall that separated the yard from the streets.

The problem was, once she got to that wall, *if* she got to that wall, there would be a brief period of time when she'd hang like a target on a hay bale.

She had genetic gifts, but she couldn't leap tall buildings in a single bound. Her heart banged with a rhythm that threatened cardiac arrest, but she didn't slow her pace.

She stifled a scream as a gunshot resounded, the bullet pinging into a container nearby. Give up, a small voice whispered inside her brain. Wouldn't a life in prison be better than being dead?

Carla Cassidy   231

"Lynn!"

She gasped at the familiar voice. Looking up she saw Nick hanging over the top of the wall. "Come on," he yelled. "I'll cover you." She'd never been so happy to see anyone in her life.

"There she is!" a voice yelled from someplace just behind her.

As she ran toward Nick he fired off a round of shots, providing the cover she needed to get to the wall. She leaped up and her fingers barely grasped the top. At the same time something clamped around her left foot.

She glanced down to see one of the dogs with her tennis shoe in his mouth. The dog shook his head and pulled, threatening to jerk her off the wall.

Her fingers trembled, threatening to slip as the dog pulled harder. "*Aufhalten! Aufhalten,*" she cried, hoping the dog would heed the command.

"Come on, come on," Nick said urgently as he fired off another round.

The dog held tight to her foot. Once again a frantic fear ripped through her as she struggled against the dog's weight and grip to get up and over the wall.

She didn't want to seriously hurt the dog, who was only doing what he'd been trained to do, but she wanted him off her.

With an effort that made her entire body tremble, she moved her leg and tried to smash the dog into the wall. Once...twice...three times and he finally yelped, released her and fell to the ground below.

She scrambled over the wall to discover that Nick had used the roof of his car to gain access to the top of the wall.

"Get in," he said, not moving from his position.

She hit the roof and quickly scrambled down and into the driver's seat. She started the engine with a roar and threw it into gear. With her foot on the brake she tensed as Nick came off the wall and flew through the passenger door.

"Go! Go!" he exclaimed.

Grabbing the wheel tightly, she tromped on the gas and headed down the nearest street. "Head for the apartment," he said. "There's no way they could see the car. We'll park it in the lot in the back."

"You weren't supposed to be here. You broke the rules."

"Yeah, breaking rules, that's another nasty habit I have," he replied.

"How did you know I was in trouble?" She shot him a sideways glance but he was half-turned in the seat, staring out the back window.

"You went silent. For a few minutes I thought you just weren't talking to me, then I realized something was wrong with the transmitter. The last thing I'd heard was the faint sound of the guards' voices then nothing."

She wheeled into a parking space next to her car in the lot and turned off the engine. "They shut me into a container." She suddenly realized he hadn't heard her report. He hadn't heard anything she'd said after she'd hit the ground. "Nick, the bomb. I found it."

"Where?" The word shot from him.

"Container 16002."

"I've got to contact Blake," he said. Together they got out of the car and hurried up to the apartment. Once there Nick grabbed his cell phone from where he'd left it on the table and dialed.

"Stingray Wharf. Mission accomplished. 16002." He repeated the information once more, then hung up.

Lynn stood at the window, half expecting police cars to roar up the block. But the streets remained deserted.

"What happens now?" She sank onto the edge of the sofa bed. Now that the adrenaline rush of danger had passed, she found herself trembling once again. That had been far too close for comfort.

"Somebody will visit the yard and the bomb will be disarmed. Nobody other than the men directly involved will ever know it was there."

She raised an eyebrow in surprise. "You mean this won't make the morning news?"

"There's no way anybody wants the people of this country to know how vulnerable the ports are despite all the efforts to make them secure." He raked a hand through his hair and his gaze was soft, tender as it lingered on her. "What happens now is you get your life back."

Leaning her head back she closed her eyes and drew

in a deep breath. It was over. She was free. She could
go back home and pick up her life where it had left off.

She pulled herself up from the sofa and went to
the table and sat in front of her laptop. "What are you
doing?" he asked as she punched the on button.

"I'm going online and I'm booking a seat on the
next available flight out of here to Phoenix." As she
made the arrangements, she consciously kept her attention on the task at hand and away from the man
who stood so near.

She'd go back to her life and he'd go back to his,
a life that included an undercover operation and a
wife. For the first time since she'd met Nick, she
realized there had never been much of a chance for
the two of them to find happiness together.

All she'd ever wanted was an ordinary life, the
kind that hundreds of thousands of people enjoyed
on a daily basis. Certainly living with Jonas had
never been ordinary.

She'd dreamed of everyday things such as sharing
coffee over a kitchen table in the mornings, working
hard and eating mac and cheese for dinner. She'd
wanted a life filled with normal worries—whether
her kids would catch the flu or if the air conditioner
would last another year.

Nick was an FBI agent and his life would always
be filled with danger and drama. There would always
be another assignment for him, another risk. An
ordinary life would never work for Nick Barnes even
if he wasn't married.

Travel arrangements made, she shut off the laptop. "I'm on a flight home at seven o'clock tomorrow evening." She looked up at him.

His features were inscrutable. "Can I take you to the airport?" She hesitated. It would be so much easier to say goodbye now. "Please, Lynn. I'd really like to see you off."

"Won't that interfere with your job?"

"I'll figure out a reason to be gone a couple of hours," he replied.

"All right," she said relenting. "Why don't you pick me up about four-thirty tomorrow afternoon." A glance at her clock told her it was after four. "And now you'd better get out of here." She was grateful he didn't try to talk about them, for there was nothing left to talk about.

"Yeah, I've got to get." He started for the door, but she stopped him by softly calling his name.

"You took a big risk, coming after me tonight. If you'd been caught you wouldn't have only been arrested, but you would have screwed up the other assignment you've been working."

"No big deal. Taking risks is what I do."

"I know." And it was the reason they could never, ever have a future together. "Still, I owe you one."

He grinned, but it was a sad kind of a grin. "Let's hope you never have to repay the favor."

Then he was gone. Lynn remained at the table, staring at the door. He was gone from the apartment and now she needed to make him gone from her heart.

At this time tomorrow night she'd be in her own bed in her own apartment. She'd done what had been requested of her and had lived to tell the tale. She should be feeling euphoric, but all she felt was a weary sadness.

It seemed that Nick did all his important thinking while driving in the car in the middle of the night and this time was no different.

When he'd heard the sounds of those guards talking so close to Lynn, his heart had stopped beating. The ensuing silence had tormented him as nothing ever had.

At first he'd thought she was just upset and wasn't talking to him, but the silence stretched endlessly and in his heart he knew Lynn was far too much of a professional to allow her anger with him to keep her still.

He'd battled with himself, his orders playing and replaying in his head. Don't interfere. Don't get involved. If she falls, she falls alone.

But ultimately he couldn't let that happen. Thank God she'd gotten out. Thank God she was safe and could go back to the life she'd been building before he and a bunch of other men had interrupted it.

There were so many things he'd wanted to say to her once they had gotten back to her apartment safe and sound. More explanations, more apologies, more attempts to make things right. But, he'd decided just to leave it alone. He loved her enough to let her go, to let her get on with her life without him.

He should have never told her he'd take her to the airport this evening. He should have said his goodbye this morning. As it was, he was just prolonging the agony.

Weariness weighed heavily on his shoulders as he drove into his driveway and got out of the car. He checked the street to make sure nobody was watching him. He hoped that if Jimmy or one of the other guys had driven by they would assume he'd been with Lynn, his mistress, while his wife slept, unaware of his infidelity.

He saw nothing to cause him concern and quickly inserted his key into the lock and opened the door. "Is everything all right?" The female voice came at him out of the darkness from the direction of the sofa.

"Jesus, you scared me half to death," he replied. He closed the door and locked it behind him. "Yeah, everything is all right now."

"I was worried. You've never been this late before."

Neither of them moved to turn on a light, not wanting to let anyone in the neighborhood know they were up and about. Still, he could easily envision her despite the darkness of the room.

Colette Branson-Barnes was a fairly attractive blond thirty-year-old, although she wasn't Nick's type at all. He preferred chestnut hair and green-gold eyes to a cool, blue-eyed blonde.

When the bureau had first approached him with the marriage scheme, he'd been reluctant. First and foremost because he'd always believed marriage was sacred and belonged to two people who loved each other.

The other concern he had was the possibility that Colette Branson would expect him to sleep with her. He didn't know the woman and worried about how it would be to live with somebody, sleep in the same bed as somebody.

Thankfully, there were no sparks, not even a hint of sexual desire between them and in the three months he'd been married to her he'd come to admire and respect her and regarded her as a friend.

"We had a few problems, but everything is okay now." He sank into the chair that faced the sofa and released a sigh. "She goes home tomorrow. That particular assignment is at an end so I won't be making any more night trips away from here."

"Is she still angry with you?"

"Probably. I'm taking her to the airport at four-thirty."

"Is that wise?" He knew she wasn't talking about his personal relationship with Lynn, but rather the assignment he was working here with her.

"I don't know. I don't know what's wise and what isn't anymore. I just want to take her to the airport. If any of the guys here question me about anything, I'll tell them I packed her off and decided it was time to seriously commit to my marriage."

He pressed two fingers against the center of his forehead where the beginnings of a headache threatened to erupt. "You should go back to bed."

"I'll just have to get up in another hour or so," she replied.

They were silent for a long moment, partners in a game with the potential for deadly consequences. "What are you going to do, Nick, when this is all over?"

"I don't know. I haven't thought about it much. What about you? You know you won't be able to stay here in town when this all goes down."

Colette had been born and raised in Raymore. She'd been the one who had initially contacted the FBI about the drug operation taking place in the town. Her help had been priceless in showing the authorities what was going on here.

However, by being a good, law-abiding citizen, she'd effectively turned her back on friends and family and when all of them were in jail cells, she'd be free, but her personal sacrifice would have been enormous.

It was possible that for the rest of her life she'd be hunted by the friends and family of the men she was helping to put away. Still, she was aware of the risks and had decided to help anyway.

"They've promised me a new identity, a life far away from Raymore, Florida. I'll start fresh and make something good out of what hasn't been such a terrific life so far."

Nick dropped his hand from his forehead. "Why'd you do it, Colette? Why did you make that call to the bureau?" In all the time they had spent together in the past three months he'd never asked her what had prompted her to come forward.

She released a sigh. "My mother was an alcoholic for as long as I can remember. But, even though she drank too much, for the most part she functioned. Then four years ago she changed vices when she discovered meth and everything went to hell. It's an evil, awful drug. Did you know that it's supposed to be more addictive than heroin?"

"Yeah, I've heard that," he replied.

"It destroyed her. She died two years ago and when I found out what was happening here, that meth was being made and distributed by members of my own family, I knew I had to do something to stop them."

"What you did was brave," he said.

"Maybe. I just know I'm ready to get it over with. I'm ready to get on with my life."

Nick nodded in the darkness, hoping they both got out of this alive so they *could* get on with their lives. He hoped like hell that Colette got her happy life in a new town.

As for his own future, he refused to think about it.

Chapter 15

Despite the late and dangerous night, Lynn awakened just after dawn. She tried to go back to sleep but instead found herself thinking over the events of the night before.

If it hadn't been for Nick running interference, she wouldn't have awakened on the sofa bed in the apartment this morning. She would have awakened in a jail cell.

He'd gone against orders, broken the rules to help her. He'd put not only his career but his life on the line for her. She'd never forget that. She'd never forget him.

Faith had mentioned Nick being her unfinished

business and that had been true. There had never been a definitive end to their relationship a year ago. Lynn felt that definitive end now.

She finally got up and padded into the bathroom for a quick shower. As she stood beneath the tepid spray, she thought of how close she had come to death the night before.

Too close. There were so many things she had yet to experience. She was still at the beginning of her journey through life and was grateful that journey hadn't ended in a bomb blast or with a bullet in the back.

Today she was going home. She'd done her job and nobody owned her anymore. Hopefully Blake would keep his promise that this was the end of it, that her record would be wiped clean and nobody would ever have anything to hang over her head again.

She dried off, dressed, then grabbed a can of diet soda from the fridge, punched on the small television then sat at the kitchen table.

As she drank her soda she watched an early-morning local news program. There had been an overnight shooting in a park, an armed robbery at a convenience store and a tragic car accident that had claimed the life of three people.

There was another tropical depression churning toward the Florida coast and was expected to hit sometime in the next five days as a category two hurricane. She'd be long gone by then.

"Some excitement last night at Stingray Wharf," the perky blond reporter announced. Lynn quickly leaned over and turned up the volume. "An intruder apparently breached security to get into the holding yard sometime early this morning but managed to escape. Our sources at the police department tell us that it was a college prank and the intruder was a young woman who sneaked into the yard on a dare. No arrests were made. And now, Kelly, let's talk about football."

Lynn turned the volume back down. She was surprised that it had made the local news, but certainly not surprised that the incident had been written off as nothing more than a silly prank.

She had no doubt that at some point during the wee morning hours men had moved in to neutralize the bomb she'd found. There would be no news about that. There would be no news of how vulnerable the ports were or how so many of them couldn't afford the equipment that would keep them secure.

Turning off the television, she switched her attention to her laptop. She had a job to do before she left here today. She was going to build Tiny his Web page advertising his church.

Keeping busy would help the hours pass and hopefully keep her thoughts from Nick. She didn't want to think about him anymore. Even if he wasn't married they wanted different things, needed different things from life.

She would tell him goodbye at the airport then she

would never, ever think of him again. She was going back to a full life in Phoenix, a life filled with friends, and her work for Oracle and her Web design business. Things would be just fine when she got home.

The first thing she did was download her e-mail, her heart beating just a little bit faster as she saw a familiar e-mail address.

She opened the message to see the familiar spiderweb design across the top right corner.

Spider bites are dangerous to tender Athena flesh.

Lynn sat back in her chair, chewed on her bottom lip and stared at the message. There was no way to view it as anything other than a threat. Just as the last one had been, this one was signed A.

Who was A and what did he or she have against the Athena women? Were the threats nothing more than e-mails, or would they escalate into something more dangerous? When she got back to Phoenix she had to contact Kim Valenti and find out who else might know that Lynn was working on the Spider files.

She forwarded the new e-mail to Delphi, then turned her attention to building a Web page for Tiny's church. As always work was a panacea for all that ailed her.

She lost herself in choosing colors and designs, then linking the page to others that would assure a good amount of traffic. By ten o'clock she had the page done. She left her place and knocked on Tiny's door.

"Who is it?" His deep voice boomed through the wooden door.

"Tiny, it's me. Lynn."

He opened the door, his broad face clad in a smile. "Hey, girl. Come on in."

She stepped just inside the door and looked around curiously. If Tiny was involved in anything illegal, he either wasn't making any money at it or chose not to spend the money on furnishings.

The apartment was sparsely furnished and spotlessly clean. A beige sofa was set against one wall and a small television rested on an entertainment center. The walls were bare except for a large picture of Jesus and there was a Bible in the center of the coffee table.

"Actually, I was wondering if you'd like to come over to my place and see your new Web site."

"Really?" His eyes lit up. "Sure. Just let me lock up." He pulled a set of keys from his pocket and together they left his apartment and went next door to hers.

"It's nothing fancy," she warned as she sat in front of the laptop. "Just a basic advertisement. If you'll give me the church's phone number I can include it on the site." She pulled up the page as Tiny peered at it over her shoulder.

"Wow, would you look at that. I like the colors. The red and gold look real nice. I don't know how to thank you, Lynn."

"No thanks are necessary," she replied. She didn't tell him she'd used Web space provided to her from her own Internet account. "If you want to write down a phone number as a contact, I'll put it in and you'll be all set."

"You sure got to this fast," Tiny said as he scribbled a phone number on a scrap of paper from his wallet.

"Yeah, well that's the other thing I wanted to tell you." She got up from in front of the computer. "I'm leaving here today."

"Leaving?" He looked at her in surprise.

"Some friends called me last night and offered me a place to stay with them in the Southwest. I've decided to take them up on their offer and I'm leaving this afternoon." She couldn't very well tell him the truth.

"I hate to see you go, but I'm glad to see you get out of this neighborhood," he said. "These friends, they're good people?"

"Very good," she replied. "I'll be okay there, Tiny. They'll take good care of me."

"Good." His keen eyes gazed at her for a long moment. "You know, I'm not sure I believe all your stories about what you're doing here and your dead rich daddy, but I won't ask you questions because I see a goodness that shines from you, Lynn."

On impulse, Lynn reached out and hugged the big man. He smelled of male sweat and cheap cologne. She stepped back from him. "You'll tell Stella goodbye for me?"

"Sure. You need a ride to the airport or anything?"

"No, I've got it covered. A friend is taking me, but thanks for the offer." A friend—that's the way she had to think of Nick. Nothing more than a friend.

Tiny smiled. "Stella's going to miss you. She won't have anyone to pick on."

Lynn laughed. "Stella's all right. Maybe someday she'll be able to leave this neighborhood and find a different kind of life."

"I'm working on it. That's part of my mission here." He offered her another smile as he headed toward the door. "Well, I'm sure you've got things to do before you catch that flight. It was nice knowing you, Lynn."

"Likewise."

She locked the door after he left and spent the rest of the afternoon packing, then working on the Spider files. She had no more success in cracking the code that had been used and was eager to get home where she had other programs loaded on her desktop computer that might be more successful.

At four o'clock she dressed in a pair of navy slacks and a long-sleeved red blouse, mindful that the planes were often cool.

She stood at the window and looked out on the streets below. She wasn't sorry to say goodbye to the view outside her window. In fact, as she waited for Nick to arrive she was struck with an intense home-sickness for cactus and roadrunners instead of palm trees and gulls.

She even had a touch of homesickness for Leo, who might ask her for sex on a daily basis but never managed to touch her heart. She had a sneaking suspicion that if she ever told Leo yes, he'd totally freak out. She was safe for him to flirt with because he knew she'd never say yes.

When she saw Nick's car pull up in front of the apartment building she didn't move from the window but rather watched him get out. The sun glistened in his dark hair and her heart clenched with the grief of what would never be. No matter how much she hated it, he would always own a little piece of her heart.

She was still standing at the window when he knocked on the door. "Come in," she called and turned to face him as he entered the apartment. "All set," she said with a forced lightness. She wanted to get this over with, wanted the goodbye to be finished without fanfare or drama.

"Is this it?" He gestured to the suitcase and briefcase that was on the floor next to the door.

"That's it."

He picked up the suitcase as she walked over and grabbed the briefcase. She kept her gaze averted from him as she did a final sweep of the room to make sure she'd left nothing behind.

It wasn't until they were on the elevator that he spoke to her again. "Lynn, I just want to tell you again that I'm sorry for hurting you. That was never my intention."

She finally met his gaze and in his eyes she saw the depths of his remorse. It seemed important that she let him off the hook, that they part ways with no regrets, no bitterness or baggage between them.

"It's okay. Last night you saved my life. I'd say you more than made up for everything else."

He flashed her a tentative smile. "I have no doubt that you would have managed to get out of the situation last night without my help. You're an amazing woman, Lynnette White."

Although she didn't argue with him she knew differently. If he hadn't shown up when he had and provided the gun cover that he had, she would have been caught or shot.

"It would have never worked anyway," she said. "You and me."

The elevator came to a halt, but he didn't move to exit. "What do you mean?"

"I mean that it's best this way, that you and I were really never meant to be. We want different things from life. I want normal. I want the picket fence and the kids. I don't want danger and undercover work and worry. Let's leave it at that, okay?"

He hesitated a moment then nodded and stepped out of the elevator.

"We made the news this morning," she said.

"Yeah, I saw the reports." He offered her a small smile, one that didn't touch the depths of his dark brown eyes. "Those crazy college students, they're always pulling some stunt or another."

They stepped outside into the afternoon sunshine to find Tiny and Stella standing just outside the building. "I came to tell you goodbye," Stella said to Lynn. "Tiny told me you were leaving this afternoon."

"I'm on my way to the airport now," Lynn replied.

She smiled at Stella, who was clad in a respectable, but worn-looking blue sundress.

Stella's gaze flickered over Nick. "That your man?"

"Something like that," Lynn replied. It was a simple question that required far too complicated an answer. She quickly made the introductions between Nick and the other two.

Stella nodded with approval. "I just wanted to tell you it was nice knowing you. And it was real nice, what you did for Tiny."

Tiny nodded in agreement. "Thanks again, Lynn." With their final goodbye said, the two turned and started up the sidewalk in the direction of the church.

"What did you do for Tiny?" Nick asked curiously as he opened the back door of his car to stow the suitcases.

"Built a simple Web page for his church."

"Nicky!"

They both turned to see Jimmy and a freckle-faced, red-haired man coming up the sidewalk toward them. She flicked a quick look at Nick and saw the stress that immediately tightened his features.

"Jimmy…Kip…what's going on? What are the

two of you doing here?" Although Nick's voice sounded perfectly calm, Lynn sensed his tension and knew this could be nothing but trouble.

"We got a problem, man." It was the redhead who spoke, the man Nick had called Kip.

"What kind of a problem?" Nick slammed the back door of his car.

"Our man wants to talk with you." Jimmy said.

"I was just on my way to take Lynn to the airport. Why don't I do that and meet you two back at my house in Raymore. We can go from there to meet the man."

"'Fraid that's not going to work. The man wants to talk to both of you." Kip's grin wasn't a pleasant gesture, but rather made him look slightly demented.

"Nick? What's going on? Who are these men and why would anyone want to talk to me?" Lynn asked, although she knew this had something to do with whatever other assignment Nick had been working.

"Is this really necessary?" Nick asked. "I mean, why get her involved at all." He pulled his car keys from his pocket. "I'll leave her at the airport and we can deal with things after that."

"I said that wouldn't work," Kip replied. With a smooth move he pulled a gun and punched it against Lynn's ribs. "You both need to come with us."

Nick's face paled as Jimmy pointed his gun at him. "Whoa, Jimmy, take it easy. You want to tell me what's going on here?"

Lynn had thought she might be able to somehow get the gun away from Kip, but there was no way she'd even try as long as Jimmy had his gun on Nick.

Even if she managed to get Kip's gun, there was something in Jimmy's eyes, a cold harshness that let her know he wouldn't hesitate to shoot Nick.

"I don't know what's going on, Nicky. I just have my orders. Now, don't make this difficult. I like you and I sure wouldn't want to do anything drastic," Jimmy said.

Drastic? As far as Lynn was concerned, pointing a Glock at a man was pretty drastic.

"Come on, we're parked across the street. And for God's sake don't do anything stupid," Jimmy said.

As they crossed the street to where a dark blue sedan was parked, Lynn wildly looked around. There were few people on the streets. Down the sidewalk she saw Tiny and Stella, both turned in her direction, but she couldn't tell if they saw what was happening or not.

"Let her go," Nick said, his voice deep with urgency as they reached the car. "I swear she doesn't know anything. If the man is worried about pillow talk, there was none. I'll come with you, but just let her go."

If the guns hadn't already told her, the intensity of Nick's plea let Lynn know they were in deep trouble. "What's going on, Nick?"

She didn't really expect an answer, but thought it wise if she continued to play stupid. Hell, it wasn't much of a stretch. She really didn't know what was happening and wished he'd been more forthcoming about the assignment he'd been working.

"Would one of you please tell me what's going on? I've got a plane to catch," she exclaimed.

"Shut up." Kip once again shoved the barrel of his gun into her ribs with a force that caused a yelp of pain to escape her.

"Hey, take it easy," Nick said, a glittering anger filling his eyes.

"I didn't hurt her none and we can't let her go, Nick. We've got our orders." He pushed her against the truck of the car. "Spread 'em, honey. I've got to make sure you aren't packing."

As he frisked her, Jimmy did the same to Nick at the front of the car. Although Lynn had no weapon, Jimmy found Nick's gun and relieved him of it.

Lynn knew that if they got into the car the odds of them getting out of this alive diminished greatly. But, before she could figure out a plan Kip used a length of rope to tie her hands behind her back, then shoved her unceremoniously into the backseat.

Within five minutes of riding in the car Nick's hands were numb from the ties that bound them together behind his back. But his mind was certainly not numb. It raced with suppositions, trying to figure out exactly how much trouble they were in.

He hoped like hell this was about the fact that they thought he'd been sleeping with Lynn. He hoped the concern was that he might have told her about what was going on in Raymore.

Certainly he didn't have to worry about her acting

ignorant about what was going on. He hadn't told her anything other than that he'd married to provide himself a deep cover.

Had his cover been blown? A trickle of cold sweat worked down his brow. If that was the case, he was dead. And worse, Lynn would be dead, as well.

There was no forgiveness for betrayal in this world.

I'm sorry, Lynn. I'm sorry I got you into this mess. He wanted to say the words out loud, let her know that he'd gladly give his own life if it meant saving hers. But, instead of speaking aloud, he half turned in his seat and looked at her, hoping his expression conveyed all that he felt.

Her face was pale, her features pinched with obvious fear. She was a smart woman, she had to know that the situation wasn't good. Besides the fear, her eyes held questions, questions he couldn't answer now.

He looked at Jimmy. "Let her go, man," he said in a low voice. "I swear, she doesn't know anything."

Jimmy frowned. "I can't, Nick. If I go against orders then I'll be dead meat. I'm sure it will all be fine. Just relax."

Yeah right, Nick thought wryly. We've got a gun trained on you and the woman you care about and we're driving you to an unknown location, but just relax.

He didn't try to change Jimmy's mind as the ride continued. He knew any attempt would be futile. All he could hope for was that when he met "the man" he'd be able to at least gain Lynn's release.

He stared out the window as they left the outskirts of Miami behind. But his mind was far away from the flashing scenery outside the window.

Did they know? Had they somehow learned he was an FBI agent? If his cover had been blown then there was no doubt in his mind that he was being driven to his death. But, somehow, someway before he died, he had to get Lynn out of this mess.

Chapter 16

With each minute of the drive, Lynn felt despair sinking deeper and deeper into her heart. Where were they being taken? What was Nick involved in?

She wished she had more information, some knowledge she could draw from to help her through this. There was nothing worse than being in danger and not knowing why.

Her shoulders joints burned from the uncomfortable position of having her hands bound behind her. But, her skin crawled each time the man named Kip looked at her.

There was an evil in his blue eyes, an evil made more pronounced by his innocent, freckle-faced features. He had the soulless gaze of a snake and each time he looked at her he smiled, an inward smile of such pleasure it made her shudder with revulsion.

She had no idea where they were. Once they had left the Miami area and had gotten on a two-lane highway, she'd lost her sense of direction. The only thing that worried her more than her own fear was the intense worry she felt emanating from Nick.

"Could somebody please tell me what's going on?" she said. She shifted positions to try to ease the strain of her shoulders.

"Jimmy, is this about Nick being married?" she asked. "Did his wife send you? Because if that's the case you can tell her she can have him. I'm through with him. He's been lying to me from the very beginning. You can tell her that she doesn't ever have to worry about me again."

"You talk too much," Kip said.

She flushed. "I'll shut up as soon as somebody tells me what's going on," she replied.

Without warning he backhanded her, the contact hard enough to spring tears to her eyes. "You'll shut up now," he said.

"What the hell are you doing?" Nick raged from the front seat. "There's no reason to hurt her. Dammit, Kip." There was a fierce intensity to Nick's tone and Lynn knew if Nick got the opportunity he'd kill Kip for what he'd just done.

"She was bugging me." Kip shrugged, his eyes gleaming with glee. "It was just a little slap."

A slap hard enough to scramble her brains, she thought. She licked her lips and tasted the tang of blood. She narrowed her eyes and stared at him. She wouldn't wait for Nick to act against him, if she got the chance she would kill him herself.

The ride seemed to be torturously long. Lynn's hands had grown numb and the burn in her shoulders had become almost unbearable.

Finally, they entered the city limits of a small town called Raymore. They drove down what appeared to be the main drag and as they did Lynn stared out the window.

A dismal place, she thought. Boarded-up storefronts were interspersed amid tattoo parlors and liquor stores, auto parts sales and a seedy-looking bar.

They passed through town and turned left on another two-lane road. They drove past a residential neighborhood of small homes needing paint and sporting ill-kept yards. After that was a trailer park, the trailers all looking as though they belonged in a junkyard.

The whole drive Lynn worked at the rope that tied her wrists together, trying to break it, somehow escape it, but her efforts were fruitless.

She sat up straighter as they turned once again, this time on a gravel road that led to a warehouse-type building. It appeared deserted. No cars were parked out front and no lights shown from any of the darkened windows that lined the very top of the structure.

What was this place? This couldn't be good. There was only one reason why men with guns would take people out to the middle of nowhere, to a warehouse where nobody would be able to hear the sound of shots.

She worked at the ropes around her wrists more frantically, afraid that this would be the place of her death, of Nick's death.

The sun was just beginning to ease down in the western sky as Jimmy parked the car in front of the door of the building.

"Okay, boys and girls, this is where we get out," 3Jimmy said.

Lynn kept her mouth shut. She didn't want to give Kip another reason to slap her. She had a feeling he was the kind of man who enjoyed slapping women around and was just waiting for another opportunity.

He used more force than necessary to yank her out of the backseat of the car again and a hint of rage overrode Lynn's fear. She welcomed the rage, knowing that she couldn't function well while afraid, but could get focused and cunning when angry.

As the four of them walked toward the door of the building, Lynn cursed the fact that Jimmy had his gun pressed firmly into Nick's back.

She had no doubt that with a well-aimed kick she could incapacitate Kip. She could kick his brains into next week and he'd never be a threat to anyone again, but she couldn't do anything while Jimmy was able to put a bullet into Nick's back.

Saving herself at the sacrifice of Nick simply wasn't an option in her world.

She'd expected a dusty, rat-infested place, but was shocked when they were led into a large room that looked like a high school science lab. The stainless steel counters, the glass beakers and other equipment made her thoughts flash back to when she'd seen Lab 33, when authorities had raided it with help from Athena women. Chills radiated out from the very center of her soul, forcing an outbreak of goose bumps on her arms.

There was evil here. She smelled it in the air just as she'd smelled it when she'd first walked into Lab 33. It was the nebulous scent of greed and desire, of crimes and immorality.

What had these men been doing in here? What terrible things had happened inside these walls? She caught a whiff of a chemical scent that she couldn't quite identify.

"What happens now?" Nick asked. It was the first time he'd said anything since Kip had slapped her.

"You wait." Jimmy motioned them both to the ground next to an exposed pipe that ran the length of the floor. "Unfortunately, we're going to have to secure you until the boss gets here."

"This isn't necessary." Nick frowned as Jimmy tied his bound hands to the pipe.

"Yes it is," Kip said as he tied Lynn's wrists to the pipe. When he was finished he stood and pulled a roll of wide silver tape from his pocket.

The sight of the tape shot a new form of terror through Lynn. She didn't want the tape slapped over her mouth. If she was going to die here, she at least wanted the opportunity to tell Nick goodbye.

She was almost relieved when Kip bent down and wrapped the tape around her ankles. When he was finished he threw the roll of tape to Jimmy, who then bound Nick's ankles together.

When both of them were secure, Kip and Jimmy stepped back from them. "You shouldn't have to wait too long," Jimmy said. "I'm afraid Kip and I have to leave you now. We've got a couple of other things to take care of."

She waited until the sound of their footsteps faded away, then she heard the clang of the door closing. It was only then she turned and looked at Nick. "Want to tell me what's going on?"

His lips were little more than a grim slash in his face.

"I don't know. It's possible my cover's been blown. All I know is we've got to get out of here now."

His face turned red with strain as he leaned forward in an attempt to wrestle his hands free. He threw his head back and squeezed his eyes closed, the muscles in his neck cording as a growl of frustration escaped him.

Lynn tried to twist and turn her hands, then concentrated on trying to break the duct tape with the strength of her legs. She strained so hard a headache crashed through her temples.

"Damn!" She finally expelled a breath, her efforts to break the silver tape to no avail. "We're not going anywhere too quickly," she said, stating the obvious.

Nick leaned his head back against the wall and released a sigh of frustration. He raised his head and looked at her once again, his eyes glittering darkly. "Maybe if we both pull up with our hands we can somehow dislodge or break the pipe."

She nodded, willing to try anything. "Okay, on the count of three. One…Two…Three! She strained upward with her hands, feeling the bite of the rope digging into her flesh.

Nick did the same, his face growing redder with his effort. The pipe didn't budge. Lynn relaxed, panting from her efforts. "I hope you have a plan B," she said.

"That was plan B," he replied dryly.

Once again her head pounded with nauseating intensity. "What is this place?" she asked. She leaned her head back against the wall and closed her eyes, willing her headache away.

"A meth lab."

She opened her eyes and turned her head to look at him. "That's what you've been working on? Some sort of a drug deal?"

"It's bigger than a simple drug deal and the last thing I wanted was for you to become involved in this in any way." She felt the anguish that shone from his eyes deep in her heart.

"I know that, but now I am involved, and I'd like to know all about it. Lord knows we need to do something to pass the time. You might as well fill me in."

He sighed wearily. "About a year and a half ago we got a call that there was a drug operation taking place in Raymore. The call came from a local woman who had an in with the men involved." They kept their voices to just above a whisper.

"I'm surprised the FBI got involved in a simple drug deal."

"Believe me, there's nothing simple about this deal. Half the people of the town are working the drugs and the other half know it's going on but look the other way."

"So, if I could scream loud enough for somebody to hear me, they probably wouldn't come to our rescue."

"That's right," he agreed. "Even the cops turn a blind eye to what goes on here. That's why we got involved, not only because of the drugs but also because of the corruption."

"So, this woman called."

"She agreed to work with us and insinuated herself as deep into the mix as she could. Jimmy is her cousin."

"Nice family tree," Lynn said wryly.

He paused a moment and she could see that he was still working to try to free his hands. He worked for several moments, then slumped in defeat. "Anyway, the woman hit a wall when it came to finding out who was behind the whole thing. We decided it was time for one of us to move in."

"You. It was time for you to move in."

He nodded. "We started setting the scene about

two months prior to me moving here. We had the woman, Colette, start talking about a guy she'd met in Miami and had fallen head over heels for, a guy named Nick Barnes."

"And I'm sure she told everybody you were the son of a mobster." Lynn knew the pain Nick had suffered at being the son of Joey Barnes. It was ironic that Joey Barnes's name had probably assured Nick a place in this drug operation.

"She did. They also knew about me working for Jonas White. I'd let them know that I was a partner in Jonas's criminal activity. But, we weren't sure if the locals would believe everything if I just breezed into town and played her boyfriend."

"So you arranged a wedding."

His gaze held hers. "Yeah, we arranged to get married in the local church by a local minister so nobody would question my commitment to Colette and my new hometown."

"And it worked." So he had been telling her the truth about the marriage.

He frowned worriedly. "I thought it had worked, but I guess we'll find out for sure in the near future." His eyes darkened and in the depths she saw raw emotion.

"Don't," she protested, a wealth of pain rising up in her chest. "Don't Nick."

"Don't what?"

"I don't want to hear any last-minute confessions. I don't want to rehash the past or mourn any future."

Once again he leaned his head back against the wall behind them. "This may be the only chance we get to talk about such things."

"They're going to kill us, aren't they?" The words tasted bad falling from her lips.

"I sure as hell hope not," he replied. "I don't know about you, but a stinking warehouse meth lab isn't my fantasy of the place where I want to die."

She leaned her head back. "Bed. I always thought it would be nice to die in my sleep when I was about a hundred years old."

"I always figured I'd go out in a blaze of glory," he replied. "Maybe in a high-speed car chase or a gun battle."

She looked at him once again. "We can't give up. I just want to figure out a way to get out of this mess."

"Let me know when you figure something out," he said darkly.

Nick had no idea how long they sat there, occasionally straining against their bonds without success. Night fell and without lights, with the windows being so high to the ceiling of the three-story structure, the interior grew dark.

As the darkness grew deeper, they began to talk once again. Despite telling him she didn't want to hash over the past, she began to talk about all the things she hadn't told him about herself, all the pieces she'd learned when she'd gone to Phoenix.

He'd known a little bit about her past, but not all of it. He listened as she told him about her mother's eggs being harvested, about those eggs being experimented with, then implanted into surrogates.

She told him her surrogate mother was a prostitute who called herself Cleo Patra. When she went into labor with Lynn, Jonas kidnapped the baby.

"And here I thought I was the one who had all the secrets," he said when she'd finished.

"Women are allowed to have secrets, men are supposed to be open books," she replied. He heard the smile in her voice and his remorse at getting her involved in this mess swooped back in to torture him.

"Is it possible we can talk our way out of this?" she asked.

"Anything is possible. I suppose it depends on how fast we can talk." He refused to give up hope. "If this is about my sleeping with you and the fear that somehow I told you too much, then we might be able to get out of it."

He'd give anything to get her out of here. He didn't want to tell her what a bad feeling he had. He knew that if the man in charge actually showed his face to talk to them, then neither of them would get out of this alive. He had too much to lose by allowing them to live if they knew who he was.

What bothered Nick as much as anything was the fact that if his cover was blown, then he must have made a mistake. And for the life of him he couldn't think of what mistake he might have made.

"What do you think is taking so long?" she asked.

Nick had been wondering the same thing. They had been in the warehouse alone for what seemed like an eternity. "I don't know." The only thing at the moment that gave him any hope at all was the fact that they were still alive.

"I thought the good guys were supposed to win."

Although he could no longer see her face, he heard the edge of fear that trembled in her voice. "We're not out yet," he said, wishing he could say something more to assure her.

Dammit, he could face the possibility of his own death, but the thought of Lynn dying here because of him made him want to weep.

Once again he strained, trying to get his hands free, but Jimmy had bound him good and tight.

"I don't suppose you had a plan C?" she asked.

"Don't make me feel worse than I already do," he replied grimly.

"Don't beat yourself up, Nick." Her voice was soft, far more forgiving than he deserved. "You couldn't have anticipated this."

"But, somehow, I feel like I should have," he replied.

"Somebody is coming," she whispered.

He tensed and a long moment later he heard the sound of the front door being unlocked. It creaked open and footsteps approached.

Overhead lights blinked on, momentarily blinding Nick with their glare. When his eyes adjusted, his heart fell to the pit of his toes.

He watched, heart pounding as Jimmy shoved the petite blonde toward him and Lynn. "Thought you two might be getting lonely," he said.

"Now are you going to tell me what's going on?" Colette asked her cousin. Even though on the surface she looked irritated and more than a little put out, Nick saw the slight tremble of one corner of her mouth and the faint edge of terror that darkened her eyes.

"Sit down and shut up," Jimmy replied.

She hesitated, then did as he told her, sliding to the floor between Nick and Lynn. "Jimmy, what's this all about?" she asked as he tied her like the other two. "For God's sake, Jimmy, we're family."

"Who is she?" Lynn asked and Nick knew she was playing the game, pretending ignorance.

"I'm Nick's wife," Colette said. "And who in the hell are you?"

"I'm Nicky's girlfriend," Lynn replied indignantly.

Jimmy laughed. "And I'll be right back and then we're all going to have a little chat."

Nick knew. He wasn't sure that Lynn and Colette knew, but he did. Their cover was blown and there was no way in hell the men working this operation were going to let the three of them leave this warehouse alive.

Chapter 17

Jimmy didn't leave the warehouse. Instead he disappeared into one of the adjoining rooms off the main room where they were all tied up.

Lynn couldn't help it—even in the midst of this life-and-death drama a strictly female reaction swept over her. She eyed the woman next to her as if they were competing for the same man.

She was pretty in a fragile, pale kind of way. She met Lynn's gaze and smiled, making her even prettier. "Don't worry, honey. It's not many women who sit in the living room on their wedding night and listen to their husband talk about the real love of his life. He's so in love with you it's disgusting."

A blush of heat swept over Lynn's cheeks. Had she been that transparent?

Colette turned her head to look at Nick. "So, what's happened? What's going on?"

"I wish we knew," Nick replied.

"It's bad, isn't it? We're busted, aren't we?" Colette whispered, voicing what Lynn had been thinking ever since she'd been tied to the damned pipe on the floor.

Somehow, Nick's cover had been blown and she'd been swept into the debris of the explosion. "Yeah, I think we're busted," Nick replied.

"Shit," Colette said succinctly.

"My sentiments exactly," Lynn agreed.

They stopped talking as Jimmy returned. He pulled up a stool and sat in front of them, looking as relaxed as if he were in a movie theater. "I think it's time for all of us to have a nice little chat," he said.

"I thought we were waiting for the man to arrive," Nick said. "You're the man, aren't you Jimmy."

Jimmy grinned. "Ah, very good Agent Barnes."

So, Nick had been right. Somehow his cover was blown. Jimmy knew he was an FBI agent. Lynn knew then that playing dumb wasn't going to work for any of them.

"I did it all, Nicky, boy. I pulled it all together, funded it with the workmen's comp check I got when I hurt my leg. I've built an empire here and I'm the king."

"You're just another two-bit dope dealer," Lynn

said in derision. What the hell, she had nothing to lose. She knew there was no way that Jimmy was going to let any of them leave the warehouse alive.

"And you're nothing but a snitch bitch who turned on her own godfather," Jimmy retorted. "Oh yeah, I know all about you. Amazing what you can find on the Internet if you know what you're looking for."

He leaned down and rubbed his leg, then straightened and smiled at Lynn. "I know how you turned on Jonas, how you worked with the FBI to bring him down. You and Colette there, you're two nasty peas in a pod, turning on your own."

"You were nothing but a snot-nosed kid before and you're nothing but a piece of crap now," Colette exclaimed angrily. "Our mothers might have been sisters, but I'm not your family."

"You got that right," Jimmy replied, a flash of anger in his eyes as he leaned forward. "You're not family. You're just one dead bitch."

"How did you know?" Nick asked. "What gave me away?"

Some of the anger died and Jimmy regarded him with a hint of respect. "I got to admit, you were good, Nicky. You didn't make any mistakes, at least none that got me suspicious. Even when I realized you were making nightly trips someplace it never really entered my mind that you might be betraying me."

"Then how did you know?"

Jimmy leaned back once again and grinned at Nick. "You got a rat in your office, Nicky boy. Even an upstanding FBI agent can crumple at the promise of cold hard cash."

As Jimmy talked, Lynn worked her legs, trying one last time to break the tape that held them together. As she strained, she felt a give. She fought back a shout of triumph, then was immediately overwhelmed by despair. Even if she managed to get her legs free, what good would that do them?

"A name. Give me a name, Jimmy," Nick said. "Tell me who you turned, who gave me up."

Jimmy hesitated a moment then shrugged. "Ah, what the hell. Agent Buzz Cantrell. For a fee he gave me all I needed to know about you and what you've been doing here."

"That bastard," Nick exclaimed.

"I'd ask you who you report to, who else knows about my little kingdom here, but it really doesn't matter."

Lynn worked her legs and felt more give in the tape. If only she could get her hands loose, work her feet loose, then she'd rip the smug Jimmy's face off.

The rope around her wrists felt looser and she moved frantically to get the rope off. If she could just work one hand out of the bonds…if she could use every ounce of strength she possessed to break the rope and free herself. At least with her hands tied behind her back Jimmy couldn't see how hard she worked to free herself.

"My operation here is finished," Jimmy continued. "I'm moving up, moving on."

"What are you talking about?" Nick asked.

"I guess it don't hurt to tell you my plans. I'm blowing this town and setting up a new shop in a little town a lot like Raymore. The people are living just above the poverty level, they have no dreams, no way to get out. I'm going to ride in like their savior and give them hope."

It was obvious Jimmy wanted them to know about all of his plans, that it was important to him that they understand just how smart he was, just how capable. It was sick. He made Lynn sick. He reached into a drawer and pulled out a black ledger book. "All good businessmen keep good records." He smiled at Nick. "Bet you'd love to get your hands on this. Unfortunately, it will perish just like you will."

"Jimmy, don't do this," Colette said. "For God's sake, let us go. Stop this madness now."

"You're right. It's time to stop the madness." He stood and shoved the stool aside. "You know I can't let any of you leave here." He looked at them one at a time, mock sadness on his face.

So this is where it ends, Lynn thought. He's going to take out his gun and execute us. She hoped he'd kill her first. She didn't want to be alive to see Nick die.

"Unfortunately, there's going to be a tragic accident here tonight," Jimmy continued. "I'm sure you all know how dangerous meth labs can be…all those chemicals. Tonight this place is going to come down." He placed a hand on the ledger. "And along with the scene of the crime, this little book will be gone, as well. Boom…and all the evidence will be gone."

Lynn stopped struggling against her bonds and stared at Jimmy. The place was going to explode? She watched as Jimmy walked over to a cabinet, opened it and withdrew an item.

She recognized it immediately from all the education she'd recently received. Primitive, easy to make and deadly. Jimmy held a pipe bomb in his hand.

"Did you know that you can find instructions for making one of these right on the Internet?" Jimmy asked. He shook his head and grinned. "Amazing. There's just enough chemicals left in the storeroom that when this goes off, they will go up and this building will come down," he said.

"You'll never get away with this," Nick said, his voice radiating with frustration. "They already have your name. They'll be looking for you."

Jimmy grinned, a good-old-boy grin that Lynn wanted to slap off his face. "Nicky boy, I've already gotten away with it. I've got enough money in an offshore account to get me a new identity, a whole new life. I'm going to buy me a town and have a new adventure."

He turned on his heels and disappeared into one of the adjoining rooms, then returned almost immediately. The pipe bomb was no longer in his hand.

"It's time for me to say goodbye," he said. "You've got an hour before all hell breaks loose. By then, I'll be long gone. And don't think anyone's going to get in here to save you. I got a nice big fat chain to lock the front door with from the outside. Those windows are way too high for anyone to get in."

"I'll see you in hell, Jimmy," Colette exclaimed.

He grinned. "Honey, you'll be there long before me." With these words Jimmy turned off the lights and left the building.

Lynn fought back a hysterical burst of laughter at the irony of life. She'd managed to escape one bomb blast only to perish in another.

Nick had never been one to give up easily, but the moment Jimmy walked out the door any lingering hope he'd entertained crashed and burned.

He knew there were enough chemicals left in those rooms to create a huge explosion. The pipe bomb would ignite it and the mix would make a fireball that nobody would be able to survive.

It was over. His work. His life. Death didn't particularly scare him, but he mourned for Lynn and Colette. Neither of them deserved this and he felt responsible for them being here.

The fact that it had been another agent who had sold him out enraged him. He knew Buzz Cantrell. They worked out of the same field office. How did a man like Buzz go to bed and sleep at night knowing he'd betrayed one of his own, knowing that he'd given in to the dark side? How much money had ex-changed hands in order for Buzz to rat him out? What had Nick's life been worth?

"I can't believe we're going to die," Colette ex-claimed, breaking the silence that had descended since Jimmy's absence.

"Maybe with three of us we can somehow break loose the pipe," Nick said. Although he had little hope of success, he didn't want the two women to know that there was no hope. "On the count of three, pull up as hard as you can with your hands. One…two…three."

They strained, groaning aloud with the effort, but the pipe remained intact. He slumped back wearily.

How many minutes had gone by since Jimmy had left? How many more minutes before that bomb exploded? An hour was nothing. Nick knew the problem with pipe bombs was that they could be unstable. Even with a timer it could detonate early.

A knot formed in his chest. "I'm sorry. I'm sorry I got you both into this."

"You didn't get me into this," Colette replied. "I got myself into this when I made that phone call to the bureau."

"Then I'm sorry I can't seem to get you out of this," he replied. Lynn was silent and he wondered what she was thinking, if she would die hating him?

"Lynn, I'm sorry for everything. I'm sorry I hurt you." Nick hadn't cried since he was ten years old and his father had taken his dog out in the backyard and shot him. But, he now felt the sting of tears pressing hot at his eyes.

His tears were for her, for the life she wouldn't have. "Lynn, I just want you to know that I love you. I love you more than I've ever loved anyone in my life." He closed his eyes, wishing the light were still on and he could see her one last time, wishing she would say something, anything.

His words filled her heart. A man about to die didn't lie. He'd been wrong not to tell her about his marriage to Colette, but she could forgive him for that.

Dammit. It wasn't fair that they should die this way. It wasn't fair that she and Nick should find each other again only to die in a stupid warehouse, blown up by a psycho dope dealer.

She wasn't just going to give up and sit in the dark and wait for that pipe bomb to explode. Even though she'd never gone to Athena Academy, she was Rainy Carrington's daughter. The blood of her mother ran in her veins. She *was* an Athena.

She thought of her sisters, all her friends and her mother's friends. Strong women. Powerful women. She dishonored them if she gave up.

Death was going to have to chase her down rather than find her sitting and waiting patiently.

Closing her eyes, she centered herself, focusing all her energy, all her concentration on the ropes that bound her wrists. She was strong. She was *Athena* strong.

In her mind's eye she saw the rope. She worked her wrists. Back and forth. Twist and turn. Ache and burn. Sweat trickled down from her hairline as she used every ounce of physical and mental strength that she possessed.

She didn't know how long she worked before she felt a significant give. She doubled her efforts and gasped in surprise as her hands came loose.

"I'm free." She nearly shouted the words as she bent forward and fumbled with the tape that held her ankles.

"You're free?" Nick's voice boomed from the darkness.

"Then get us free," Colette nearly sobbed. "Oh God, hurry."

"I just have to get this tape off my ankles." She cursed as her fingers trembled, making them all feel as clumsy as thumbs.

She ripped at the tape and finally managed to free herself. She needed light. She couldn't see in the dark to untie Colette and Nick.

She raced to the switch on the wall and flipped it on, flooding the place with welcoming light. "There should be a knife or something sharp in one of those drawers," Nick said tersely. He jerked his head toward the cabinets.

Certainly it would be quicker if she could cut them loose rather than attempt to untie their knots.

She ran to the cabinets and tore open first one drawer and then another, seeking anything that could be used to cut through rope.

Seconds ticked by. She didn't want to think about what they would do when they were all free. According to what Jimmy had told them, the front door wasn't an option as an escape route and the windows were so high nobody would be able to reach them.

They'd figure something out, she thought. In the fourth drawer she checked, she found a razor blade. She grabbed it.

"Colette first," Nick said. "Hurry, Lynn. For God's sake, hurry."

She had only taken two steps toward Colette when a loud crash rent the air. The lights flickered off and Lynn froze and squeezed her eyes tightly shut and waited for the blast that would blow her apart.

Chapter 18

No blast.

Lynn opened her eyes to see twin headlights and the front end of a very familiar Buick smashed through what had been the door to the warehouse.

As she watched in stunned surprise, Tiny opened the driver's side door and Stella got out of the passenger door. Sheetrock dust filled the air and the front end of the car hissed steam from a ruptured radiator. Lynn had never been so happy to see anyone in her life.

"Are you all right?" Tiny yelled.

"We've got to get out of here. There's a bomb in the place," Lynn exclaimed. She ran over to Colette and began to cut her loose.

Stella ran to Nick and pulled a small but wicked-looking knife from her pocket. As Lynn worked to free Colette, Stella sawed on Nick's ropes.

Colette got free and quickly tugged on the tape that bound her ankles. "Hurry, Stella," Lynn said frantically.

"Cool it, girlfriend, I'm working as fast as I can."

"Lynn, get out of here now," Nick said urgently.

As Nick's hands came free, Stella tucked the knife back in her dress pocket. "Go, go, all of you. I'm right behind you," Nick yelled as he ripped at the tape on his feet.

Chaos followed. Lynn followed Tiny up and over the hood of the car to get out of the warehouse. Once outside Lynn heard sirens in the distance as the five of them ran away from the building, which might explode at any moment.

"That would be the cavalry," Tiny said.

"If that's the local cops, then they aren't coming to help," Lynn exclaimed.

"I didn't call the Raymore cops," Tiny replied with disgust. "I hear things about Raymore. I called a friend of mine with the Miami police."

"And I called the FB and I," Stella added proudly. "Told them my two friends, Lynn White and Nick Barnes, had been kidnapped right off the street."

"We saw those men force you into their car, so me and Stella got into my car and followed. We didn't know what was going on, but we knew you were in trouble." In the moonlight Tiny's face looked as menacing as Lynn had ever seen it. "We waited and watched. When we finally saw that man chain shut the front door and leave, we decided it was time to call the authorities and come in." He grimaced. "We didn't know if we'd find you dead or alive."

The sirens grew louder as half a dozen cars came barreling down the gravel road toward the warehouse. Lynn closed her eyes and dropped down to the ground as she breathed deeply of the sweet-scented night air.

They'd made it. Thank God, they'd all made it out alive.

She heard the sound of cars screeching to a halt and the slam of doors. Wearily she stood up from the tall grass where she'd momentarily sought refuge.

There was chaos as everyone began talking at once.

Colette was explaining to a tall, dark-haired agent about the bomb, the drugs and Jimmy. Tiny was telling a shorter man about how he and Stella had seen the kidnapping and had followed them here.

Lynn looked around. The one person she didn't see in the crowd of men was Nick. "Nick?" She called his name. There was no reply.

She walked over to Colette. "Have you seen Nick?"

"Yeah, a minute or two ago," Colette said. "I saw him hurrying back toward the warehouse."

"We need to back these cars up," one of the agents yelled. "We all need to back up from the building."

Lynn looked back at the warehouse, her blood roaring in her ears. Had he gone back in to save some crucial evidence? Oh God. *The ledger.*

"Oh no." She took a step toward the warehouse, then another.

"Hey!" A deep voice yelled from someplace behind her.

She knew he was in there.

Before she could take another step forward, large burly arms wrapped around her. "What the hell are you doing?" A deep voice exclaimed. "We've got to get back."

"Please, he went back inside." She looked up at the big agent who held her tight. "Nick went back into the warehouse. We've got to get him out of there." She struggled but he held her tight. "Let me go!"

At that moment there was a loud explosion. Almost immediately a rumble began, a rumble that shook the ground where they stood. The building erupted.

The agent who had hold of her yanked her to the ground and covered her body with his as burning and thick debris rained down on them.

"No," she whispered into the ground as a deep, wrenching sob ripped through her. "No!" She screamed the word in protest.

The rain of fire, chunks of concrete and other rubble seemed to last forever. When it was finally over, the agent got off her and pulled her to her feet.

"Are you all right?" he asked.

She stood and looked toward where the warehouse had once stood. It was a fiery pile of nothing.

There was no way anyone who had been inside could have survived. No, she wasn't all right. She wasn't sure she would ever be all right again.

It was an endless night. Eventually Lynn and the others were transported away from the scene and taken back to an FBI field office in Miami.

Statements were made and remade. Lynn talked to first one, then another agent and through it all she remained numb. Nick was gone and her grief was too great for tears. She told the agents about Buzz Cantrell and was assured he'd be arrested immediately.

It was near dawn when finally the questions had been answered, the reports had been made and they were all released.

She stood outside the field office with the morning sun just beginning to peek over the horizon. Tiny, Stella and Colette exited the building along with the agent who was driving them home.

She forced a tired smile at Tiny and Stella. "I don't know how to thank you both," she said. "You put your own lives on the line for ours." She went up on her toes and kissed Tiny's cheek.

Tiny shrugged, looking a bit embarrassed. "I only did what a good Christian should do in coming to the aid of my sister."

"You kiss me and we're gonna have problems," Stella exclaimed. "I might be a hooker but I sure don't swing that way." Stella grinned and touched

Lynn's hand lightly. "You take care of yourself, girlfriend."

Lynn nodded, then looked at Colette. Her blond hair was still covered with dust and grime and the strain of the night shone from her red-rimmed blue eyes.

Lynn's chest tightened as Colette stepped toward her and wrapped her arms around her. The two women hugged tight for a long moment. When Colette finally released her and stepped back, her face was shiny with tears.

"How funny is this?" she said, swiping at her cheeks. "Nick's wife hugging his mistress." With almost tenderness she reached out and placed a hand on Lynn's shoulder.

"Mourn him," she said softly. "Mourn him and then let him go. He loved you so much, Lynn. He'd want you to find happiness."

The vise in Lynn's chest grew even tighter.

"You sure you don't want a ride somewhere?" an agent asked her.

She shook her head as Colette stepped away from her. "No, I'll be fine," she said.

She watched as they all got into a car. A moment later the car pulled away from the curb and disappeared from her sight.

The sun splashed colors across the sky, promising a beautiful day. As she raised her face toward the warmth of the sun, the numbness that had protected her from her grief fell away.

Sharp jagged pain tore through her, threatening to double her over. *Nick*, her heart cried. Oh, Nick. Even though she had known she'd tell him goodbye, she'd never expected it to be like this. She had never, ever expected death to orchestrate their final goodbye.

As the first spurt of tears filled her eyes, she drew a deep breath and took off running. She pumped her legs and swung her arms, falling into a rhythm as the blessed cocoon of numbness enveloped her once again.

She ran until she could run no more, then she stopped and rested. When she'd caught her breath she got up and ran some more.

She was afraid to stop, afraid to slow down, certain that when grief finally caught up with her she would surely die from it.

It was just after noon when she reached her final destination. She stopped on the street corner just across from her apartment building to once again catch her breath.

Nick's car sat at the curb, just as it had when she and Nick had been forced away from it at gunpoint. A young man sat on the hood, reading a book and sipping from a two liter bottle of pop.

She recognized him as the young man she'd seen at the church. Jessie. That was his name. He was the teenager whom Tiny was mentoring.

As she walked across the street he looked up and quickly jumped off the hood. "Hey," he said, apparently recognizing her.

"What are you doing here, Jessie?" she asked.

"Tiny told me to watch the car and make sure nobody stole the stuff out of it." She leaned forward enough to see her suitcase and briefcase in the backseat, just where Nick had left them. "I didn't touch anything," he said hurriedly, as if afraid she might accuse him of something.

"Of course you didn't," she replied and forced a smile. "Hang on and I'll get you some money." She opened the back door and pulled out her briefcase.

"Nah, Tiny would skin me alive if I took anything from you." He grabbed his pop and his book. "Tiny says sometimes you do things just 'cause it's the right thing to do." He offered her a shy smile. "I figure this is one of them."

His kindness was nearly her undoing. She blinked back tears as he took off down the sidewalk. She grabbed both her briefcase and the suitcase and carried them inside the building.

The FBI had arranged for her to be on a flight later that evening back to Phoenix. She had the afternoon to kill before she had to leave for the airport.

Wearily she leaned against the wall as the elevator carried her up to the third floor. She dug the keys out of her briefcase and unlocked the apartment door.

She dropped the bags just inside the door, then locked it and collapsed on the sofa. It was only then that the numbness once again fell away and she wept.

Chapter 19

"Leo, get your hand out of my pumpkin," Lynn exclaimed and scowled at the big man.

"I'd like to put my hand on your pumpkin," he said. He grinned wickedly as he pulled his hand out of the bright orange plastic pumpkin that sat next to the front door, ready for the little munchkins who should begin appearing at any moment.

Lynn rolled her eyes. "It's hard to take a man dressed like a lima bean seriously."

Leo rubbed a hand across his green face. "You got to admit, it's pretty ingenious. I mean, how many lima beans do you see on Halloween night?"

"You need to get a real girlfriend, Leo," she said.

"Maybe find a girl lima bean to talk to instead of sexually harassing your neighbor to pass the time."

"I'll get a girlfriend when you get a boyfriend," he countered. The wicked gleam in his eyes faded and he gazed at her seriously. "You need to get a life, Lynn. Ever since you got back from your vacation all you do is stay cooped up in this place and work."

"I have a life," she protested. "And stop looking so worried. It's totally out of character for you. There's nothing worse than a worried lima bean."

He smiled and dropped his hand once again into the plastic pumpkin. He pulled out a miniature candy bar and held it out to her. "Here, eat this. I hear that chocolate is good for what ails you."

She forced a laugh and took the candy bar from him. "Now, get out of here. I don't want you scaring away my little trick-or-treaters." She gave him a shove toward her door.

"Okay, okay. I'm going. Pizza Saturday night?"

She hesitated. They hadn't done a pizza night since she'd gotten back from Florida. "I don't know. We'll see," she said, unwilling to commit.

He gave her a jaunty salute, then left. She closed the door after him, then walked to her window and peered outside. Halloween night. The sidewalks should begin crawling with little ghosts and goblins at any time.

There was nothing that could appear on a Halloween night that would scare Lynn. After what she'd lived through in Florida, she didn't think she'd ever know real fear again.

She moved from the window to the sofa and sat, thinking of Leo. She hadn't told him about Nick, hadn't shared with him the utter devastation she'd brought home with her from the trip. She knew he suspected something horrible had happened, but thankfully he hadn't pried.

He was right, she hadn't done much of anything but work since she'd come home. For the first week she'd hardly been able to function. Her sorrow over Nick had been so all-consuming. It still was.

Nick's death had made the national news, not just because he'd been an FBI agent who had died in the line of duty, but also because he'd been the eldest son of reputed mobster Joey Barnes.

There had been a memorial service in Florida for Nick four days after the explosion. Lynn hadn't gone. Her pain had been too huge for a public ceremony. Instead, she had spent the day on her sofa, wrapped in a grief more deep, more dark than she'd ever known.

It had been on that day that Faith had called. God bless Faith and her psychic abilities. She had known Lynn was in a bad way. She had immediately hopped a plane and stayed with Lynn for three days.

And in those three days she encouraged Lynn to talk about Nick, to tell her everything that had happened, to vent all the emotions Lynn had tried so hard to suppress.

It had been a cathartic three days and at some point during that time with her sister's support and love, Lynn had taken a first step on the road to healing.

Although she hadn't talked to Tiny since being home, she'd used some of the money the FBI paid her to make a substantial anonymous donation to his church.

Even though she'd made it anonymously, she had a feeling that Tiny would know where it came from. She hoped he'd use some of the money to help Stella find a different line of work and the start of a new life.

She'd been debriefed by Blake, who hadn't answered many of her questions, but who had assured her that the FBI was working on finding the intended destination of the bomb and the specific mastermind behind the plot.

She'd managed to decipher another list of names from the file and had sent it on to Delphi. She'd met Kim Valenti for dinner one evening and was pleased to discover that they had a lot in common. She had a feeling over the coming months Kim might become a new good friend.

She had received no further e-mails from A, but had a feeling she hadn't heard the last from the spider source. All in all, she'd managed to reclaim her life here, but she knew it would be a long time before she could do as Colette had encouraged her and find any real happiness.

By seven, her doorbell rang on a regular basis and for the next two hours she enjoyed handing candy out to babies dressed as lambs and bugs, young girls clad in princess gowns and boys proud in superhero attire.

Although she loved seeing the children, loved the sound of their innocent giggles and the gift of their shy little smiles, she also saw what might have been in every baby face.

If Nick had lived would they have managed to find a way to meld their lives together? Her grief nearly overwhelmed her.

She wished she hadn't been on the pill when they'd made love. She wished she'd gotten pregnant and now carried his child. It was a purely selfish wish. On an intellectual level she never would have wanted a child growing up without a father. But on a strictly emotional level, she wished she had a piece of Nick that had been left behind, a legacy that would have survived his death.

By nine o'clock her doorbell had stopped ringing. It was a school night so Lynn assumed most of the kids had been filled with candy and tucked into bed.

She turned off her porch light and locked the door. Even though it was early, she intended to call it a night. Her heart felt unusually heavy and she was ready for the sweet oblivion of sleep.

It took her only minutes to wash her face and change from her jeans and T-shirt into one of her silky nightgowns. She was going from the bathroom to the bedroom when the doorbell rang once again.

So, maybe not all the trick-or-treaters were in bed, she thought as she pulled on a robe and hurried to the door. She flipped on the porch light and pulled open the door, plastic pumpkin in hand.

A bad joke. That's the first thing she thought when she saw the man who stood on her porch. Somebody was playing a horrible joke.

Despite the fact that his hair was a light brown and his eyes were green instead of that deep, dark chocolate, the man on her porch looked amazingly like Nick.

Her brain couldn't wrap around it. Had somebody dressed up on Halloween to look like Nick?

And then he spoke. "Lynn," he said softly.

The plastic pumpkin dropped from her hand. "Nick?"

"Yeah, baby. It's me."

A miasma of emotions railed inside her, the dominant one exploded into anger. She launched herself at him and beat on his chest with her fists as tears of relief flooded from her.

He did nothing to deflect her blows, but just stood there and allowed her to beat his chest until she'd flailed herself out. Only then did she wrap her arms around him and held on tight, as if afraid this was a dream and when she woke up he'd be dead once again.

He crushed her to him and she drew in the familiar scent of him, wept tears of joy, then finally shoved back from him and eyed him angrily. "You're supposed to be dead," she cried. "I mourned for you. Damn you, Nick! I saw that warehouse blow up and thought you were in it."

"Can I come in?"

She realized they were standing in the doorway and she pulled him inside and slammed the door. She wanted answers. Dammit, she deserved answers. "I have just spent the last three weeks of my life mourning the death of the man I loved. I thought you were dead!"

"Nick Barnes is dead. He died in that warehouse explosion." He took her hand and led her to the sofa, where he sat then pulled her down next to him. "I had to die, Lynn. Nick Barnes had to die that night if I was going to have any kind of a life afterward."

"I don't understand. What are you talking about?" Up close she could see that he had on colored contact lenses. His hair color had been lightened and suddenly she did understand. "The Witness Protection program?"

He smiled and her heart swelled. There was no way he could disguise the smile that had always melted her heart. "Allow me to introduce myself," he said. He took her hand in his. "My name is Frank...Frank Torrell."

"Nice to meet you, Frank," she replied. She frowned and studied him. "Oh Nick, what happened that night? Where were you when the warehouse blew up?"

His smile fell away and he stood as if unable to sit still as he told her what had happened. "I ran outside and realized that we needed the ledger to take Jimmy and his entire operation down. It was sitting under the bomb. I grabbed it with seconds left and almost didn't make it out—and when I did, my supervisor grabbed me and took me away from the scene."

"But why?"

"Because Nick Barnes had outlasted his usefulness to the bureau. Because they knew it was time for me to get out, that I wanted out. So, it was a perfect opportunity. The only way I could have a life was to die."

"Couldn't you have told me? Couldn't you have somehow contacted me?" She stood, too agitated to stay seated. As she thought of the last three weeks she wanted to hit him again. Instead she clenched her fists at her sides and bit her bottom lip.

"I couldn't. I had to let it all play out." He raked a hand through his hair and held her gaze intently. "I seem to spend a lot of time apologizing to you. And you have every right to be angry. You have every right to hate my guts, but, Lynn, I had to see this through before I could let you know what had happened."

Her fingers unclenched as she realized she couldn't maintain any real anger toward him. She was too damn glad he was alive to be mad that he wasn't dead.

He began to pace. "I haven't exactly been on a vacation for the last three weeks. I've been working with the bureau to arrest all the men who were part of the meth operation."

"And Jimmy?" she asked.

"Was arrested yesterday in a small town in Kansas and is now behind bars and charged with enough criminal offenses to keep him in prison for the rest of his life. I had to wait until that was done before I could come here."

He stopped pacing and once again looked at her. "Lynn, when you left me last year I went a little crazy. I threw myself into my work and when they approached me about the marriage, I figured what difference did it make? You were gone and by then we weren't even in contact. If I wasn't married to you, then I didn't care who I was married to."

It wasn't until that moment when she looked at the expression on his face, when she saw the depth of emotion shining from his eyes, that she realized how deeply she'd hurt him when she'd left.

"Anyway, I had to finish all that business before I came here," he continued.

"And why are you here now?" Her heart beat unsteadily.

He grinned that wonderful smile again. "I brought you presents."

She laughed. "I hope it's not aerial shots of some shipyard or a radiation scanner."

"Nah, these presents are better than any I've ever brought you before." He reached into his pocket and pulled out a pack of unopened cigarettes and laid them on the coffee table. "I had three nasty habits when this all went down. This was one of them that I've now quit."

She frowned. "You came all the way here to tell me you've quit smoking?"

"That's just the beginning," he replied. "My

second nasty habit was that I often broke the rules and didn't do what my supervisor instructed me to do. That's no longer going to be a problem because Frank Torrell doesn't have any supervisors."

"So, what is it that Frank Torrell does?" she asked with a touch of impatience.

"I don't know yet, but it's going to be something safe, something normal." He reached into his pocket and a sheet of paper folded in half. He handed it to her.

"That's your criminal record. Clean. Unfortunately they refused to remove your speeding tickets, but everything else is gone." His gaze was soft, tender. "They can't hold your past over your head ever again, Lynn."

"Thank you," she murmured. "But, you didn't have to hand deliver this." She looked at him searchingly.

"Ah, but I did," he replied. He took a step toward her. "I have one other habit and I've tried my best to break it, but I can't." His eyes glittered with an emotion that shot warmth through her limbs.

"And what habit is that?" she asked. Her mouth felt too dry as he moved so close to her that she could feel his warm breath on her face, smell the wonderful scent of him that had long ago burrowed deeply into her heart.

He reached out and stroked a strand of her hair, then ran his finger down her cheek. "The crazy, seemingly impossible to break habit I have of loving you."

He leaned his head down to cover her lips with his and she welcomed the kiss. He gathered her into his arms and once again tears fell from her eyes…tears of joy.

When the kiss ended he looked at her with an intensity that spoke of his love. "You told me in the elevator before we were kidnapped that you wanted a normal life."

She nodded, holding her breath. "I want that normal life with you, Lynn. I want a house with a picket fence and kids playing in the yard and the most dangerous thing going on in our lives is drinking coffee in the morning that's too hot."

She smiled up at him, loving him. "I think I'm going to like you, Frank Torrell. In fact, if you give me just a minute I think I could be head over heels in love with you."

"I'll do better than give you a minute. I'll give you the rest of my life if you'll have me."

Fear shone from his eyes, a fear even greater than the one she'd seen on the night they'd nearly died. She realized he was afraid she might not give them a chance.

"Aren't you afraid that being with me might put you at risk?" she asked.

"As long as Nick Barnes remains dead, there's no reason for anyone to come looking for me or for you."

"It's going to take you the rest of your life to make up for what you put me through these last three weeks," she said.

The fear fled from his gaze as he once again wrapped her in his arms and kissed her. She didn't have the heart to tell him that she thought they were both probably unrealistic fools for thinking their life together could be anything close to normal.

She was working on decoding files for a secret agency and receiving threatening e-mails from a person known as A. And that didn't even take into account what Frank Torrell might decide to do with his life.

No, ordinary and normal was probably out of the question for them. It was going to be an adventure and all Lynn knew for certain was that she was going to go along for the ride.

* * * * *

The women of ATHENA FORCE
aren't done yet!
Don't miss next month's adventure,
COMEBACK *by Doranna Durgin.*
Available August 2006
wherever Silhouette Books are sold.

If you enjoyed what you just read,
then we've got an offer you can't resist!

Take 2 bestselling
love stories FREE!
Plus get a FREE surprise gift!

Page-turning drama...

Exotic, glamorous locations...

Intense emotion and passionate seduction...

Sheikhs, princes and billionaire tycoons...

This summer, may we suggest:

THE SHEIKH'S DISOBEDIENT BRIDE

by Jane Porter

On sale June.

AT THE GREEK TYCOON'S BIDDING

by Cathy Williams

On sale July.

THE ITALIAN MILLIONAIRE'S VIRGIN WIFE

On sale August.

With new titles to choose from every month,
discover a world of romance in our books written
by internationally bestselling authors.

HARLEQUIN *Presents*

It's the ultimate in quality romance!

Available wherever Harlequin books are sold.

BOMBSHELL™

COMING NEXT MONTH

#101 HAUNTED ECHOES by Cindy Dees
The Madonna Key
Assigned to recover a stolen Madonna statue with mysterious powers of life and death, Interpol art expert Ana Reisner and her sexy art-thief-turned-professor partner fell prey to strange visions, ghostly visitations and even a bogus murder rap. Soon time was running out, as the thieves' misuse of the relic threatened to bring a nation to its knees....

#102 COMEBACK by Doranna Durgin
Athena Force
Less than a year after defusing a hostage crisis, Selena Shaw Jones was back in the Middle East to find a missing ex-terrorist and his case officer—her own husband, Cole Jones. Could Selena overcome traumatic memories of her last mission and the mistakes of her current partner to recoup the men...and avert a major strike against America?

#103 TRACE OF DOUBT by Erica Orloff
A Billie Quinn Case
Forensic pathologist Billie Quinn's TV appearance in a rape case drew unwanted attention from an unexpected quarter—the serial killer who'd murdered her mother all those years ago. Now Billie turned to the DNA to catch a cold-case killer—but would revisiting the doubts of her past save her in the here and now?

#104 DETOUR by Sylvie Kurtz
Hard-driving private investigator Sierra Martindale was at the top of her game—until she needed a heart transplant. But this second lease on life came with an unwanted side effect—being haunted by nightmares about being murdered! Soon recovery took a back seat, as Sierra took a detour to Texas...to hunt down her heart donor's killer.

SBCNM0706